TURNED AWAY

The World War II Diary
of Devorah Bernstein

BY CAROL MATAS

Scholastic Canada Ltd.

WINNIPEG, MANITOBA
DECEMBER, 1941

December 6, 1941

Is it wrong to be happy?

Daddy says that's a "big question" and that I am always asking big questions. "Couldn't you ask me why leaves turn yellow in the fall, or something easy?" he asked me at dinner tonight.

I had come home from ballet class full of happy feelings. Mrs. Roberts had actually praised my pirouettes. I couldn't believe it! Praise from Mrs. Roberts, as you know, dear diary, is as rare as rain in Winnipeg in December. I waited for the streetcar, floating on air. But when I got home and flopped down on my bed, the first thing I saw was Sarah's letter, lying there on my pillow where I'd left it when I hurried off to class. How could I have forgotten Sarah's plight, even for a few hours, and allowed myself to be so happy? Her letter makes me feel like crying. But I know that soon I'll feel happy again. Is there something wrong with me?

I am going to paste her letter in here so I don't lose it and so she becomes part of us, dear diary. And since this is my first entry in a brand new diary, I think it's a good way to start.

2 rue d'Andigne,
Paris, France
November 1

Chère Devorah,

I know that there is no use living in the past, but I can't help but remember our wonderful last visit. We were children then, four years ago, but so happy and carefree. And when I think that perhaps we could have found a way to stay with you in Canada, I find myself crying. Remember when we swam at Winnipeg Beach? Remember Adam throwing us up in the air so we'd splash into the water? Remember playing baseball with Morris and his friends and me picked last, so I cried? To think that was my biggest worry then. Remember Rachel and Adam getting in trouble because they went to a party and stayed out too late? And remember us walking with the entire family at sunset along the beach, the white sand soft beneath our feet, the dunes rising like soft pillows around us, the sky orange and red and purple and the two of us holding hands? And the corned beef sandwiches we ate at Oscar's — ten feet high!! And the hot dogs and chips from Kelekis. My mouth waters just thinking about it. Food is so scarce here. Do you still go to Kelekis now that you live in a different part of the city?

I'm very glad that your mother was so brave all

*those years ago and travelled from France to Canada
to see the world. And I'm so glad that she and your
papa met and that she stayed in Canada. Otherwise
we would have no relatives there and no hope! I know
that sounds selfish, but at least with you working to
get us over there we can live in hope. Without hope
what is there? Strange how different my papa and
your mother are, especially when they are brother and
sister. Papa is so reluctant to do anything out of the
way. Rachel takes after your mother, though, not my
papa. Me, I'm afraid I'm more like Papa.*

*I dwell on the past in this letter because I dread
telling you what the present is like. To live under the
rule of those who hate you, pass them in the street and
know they despise you simply because you are Jewish, it
is hard to bear, day in and day out. We live in fear, a
vague all-encompassing fear that is hard to describe.*

*I told you about the thousands of Jews who were
rounded up in August, many of them lawyers. And
we are beginning to hear such strange rumours about
what is happening to the Jews who are taken away.
But I will not even repeat them. They are surely just
that, rumours by people afraid of what might be in
store for us.*

*Papa is still trying to get us visas to come to
Canada and he says your parents are working hard
on that front and that we must not give up hope. I*

will keep hoping. Why does Canada not want us, that's what I don't understand. Surely Canada needs more people like Papa. And I'm sure Maman could be useful as a teacher there, correct? And Rachel is clever and I'll be a great pianist and since Maman spoke English to us when we were young, we don't even have accents — well, barely — and therefore, we'd be excellent citizens. She always says she did it because she believed it was good for our brains to speak many languages, but how fortunate it may turn out to be.

Well, I'll try to write again next time Papa sends a letter to your parents, even though you must now dread receiving my letters, as they are so full of gloom. I know! For my next letter I'll try to think of all the good things — perhaps that will help me to look on the bright side.

Keep me in your prayers. You will always be my dearest friend and cousin,

Sarah

Last week Mommy told me that a month ago the Germans blew up eight synagogues in Paris. That same day she showed something, a paper, to Daddy, but wouldn't let me see it. I overheard her saying that she translated it from one of the French newspapers. I found the scrap of paper on a side table in the living room a few days ago. I'm going to paste it in here too. Because later when I tell my children they simply won't believe me that such awful things could have been said, will they?

Death to the Jew! Death to meanness, to deceit, to Jewish wiles! Death to the Jewish cause! Death to Jewish usury! Death to all that is false, ugly, dirty, repulsive, Negroid, cross-bred, Jewish! Death! Death to the Jew! Yes. Repeat it. Death! D.E.A.T.H. TO THE JEW! For the Jew is not a man. He is a stinking beast. We defend ourselves against evil, against death — and therefore against the Jews.

You can see why I worry about being happy, dear diary. I mean, after reading this you'd think I'd never crack a smile again and yet, one happy afternoon and all my cousin's suffering is forgotten. And all the hatred directed against her — and if I admit it, me, because I'm Jewish too. And it's not only my cousin Sarah. What about my very own brothers? I have Adam in England to worry about, and Morris in Hong Kong. Maybe there *is* something wrong with me. Maybe I'm heartless!

LATER

At dinner I asked Mommy and Daddy what they were doing to get Sarah and her family over here. They said that they have called the people at the Canadian Jewish Congress and that they were told that the Congress is working as hard as they can to get Jews over here. Sarah's letter came tucked into a larger envelope with a letter from Uncle Nathaniel addressed to Mommy, and I think they are using Uncle Nathaniel's information to help them convince the authorities about the plight of the Jews overseas. And of course Daddy has written the prime minister. Daddy explained to him all about our family in France and told him what good citizens they would be if they were allowed to immigrate, and pleaded with him to be generous — as we know Canadians are. So far though, it seems as though our government just doesn't care. I can't understand that. How can they *not* care? I feel like writing the prime minister myself and asking him why they don't like Jews. Maybe I will!

Daddy has told Uncle Nathaniel to pretend he is Christian and to try to get a visa that way, but Uncle Nathaniel says things are not that desperate yet. I read them some of Sarah's letter and asked what could be more desperate? Daddy said, "You must understand, Devvy, that your Uncle Nathaniel was a judge on the high court in Paris until he was fired because of being Jewish. He only travelled in the most elite circles of society. He simply doesn't believe that a *gendarme* would have the gall to arrest him. I hope he's right."

"But the Nazis don't care about that, do they?" I asked.

Mommy answered, "All the Nazis and the *gendarmes* care about is whether Uncle Nathaniel is Jewish — not who he is, or what he has accomplished. They would probably enjoy bringing him down from his 'high horse.'"

It all makes me feel so helpless. I wish I could wave a magic wand like the good witch in *The Wizard of Oz* and make things better. Or throw a bucket of water over Hitler and see him melt. Or drop a house on him!

DECEMBER 7

Dear Diary,

I am hiding in my bedroom, away from Mommy and Daddy and the tears. When I went downstairs for breakfast I found Daddy and Mommy sitting at the table with Uncle Simon and Auntie Adele, poring over an extra edition of the paper. Here's the headline: JAPANESE DECLARE WAR ON GREAT BRITAIN AND U.S. The Japanese have attacked the Americans in Hawaii at their base called Pearl Harbor. An editorial says that on balance the attack is probably a good thing because at least the Americans will now be in the war.

Here's a direct quote from the front page: *Our*

Canadian troops, including Manitoba men, at Hong Kong, will be in the front line of battle. I'm so worried I'm shaking and can barely write. Why did Morris and cousin Isaac have to sign up? Why?

In fact, I have Morris's last letter to me here somewhere — so I'll paste that in. The thing is, diary, the boys based in Hong Kong were just sent there for show. That's what Morris told me and what Mommy has kept telling me. "Don't worry," she'd say, "no one is going to attack them there." So much for that!

Here's Morris's last letter:

The Winnipeg Grenadiers
November 20th, 1941

My dear Dev,
Well, we are finally off the boat. What a trip it was. We arrived here on the 16th. The sun was shining, even though the mountains were still surrounded by mist. We travelled on a ship called the Awatea. *A lovely boat but they put triple the number of soldiers on it than it was meant to hold! We lost men on the trip who jumped ship, things were so bad — but it wasn't that bad for me because I always had Isaac to tease and he me, so we kept in good spirits. We landed at Kowloon, the city on the mainland here. Victoria is on the island. Well, dear sister, just go look it up on a map. At any rate, what a city! The*

most extreme opulence and the worst poverty.
We marched past beggars and we marched past
Mandarins — yes, really, wearing purple robes.
And the British, of course, in their white suits, being
carried about in rickshaws.

We are stationed in the Shui Po Barracks. There
are about 40 of us in the barracks and guess what?
We have servants! Can you imagine me with a
servant? I always remember you saying to me, I'm not
your servant! Well, before I'm even really awake one
of the 3 batmen assigned to us is shaving me in bed!
Now, don't laugh. I almost have enough hair on my
face to shave. And my bed is made and my clothes
laid out. Tell Moms that I will be spoiled rotten by
the time I get home. But I must admit that these
servants make me a little nervous — because they are
Chinese — and when I'm being shaved I wonder if
they just let the knife slip a little…you see, some are
hoping for the Japanese to come and save them. Fifth
columnists, we call them. Bizarre logic when you
think that the Japanese and Chinese are enemies —
but some Chinese would still prefer life under the
Japanese than life under the British. Anyway, I hope
you like the little trinket I've enclosed. I want to
impress you by how much it cost but can't resist
telling you how little it cost — a nickel!

You never worry, Dev, but I know Moms does. So

just tell her I'm fine and that Isaac is as annoying as
ever. He immediately gave all the money he had on
him to the children begging in the streets, and so now
I need to support him. But what else is new? He'd
give away his uniform if I weren't here to stop him.
Lots of love to the family.
Have you heard anything from Adam lately?
Morris

Morris doesn't fool me. If Isaac gave away his money I'm sure Morris was right behind him. They are both such softies. I can't imagine them fighting, and with guns. It makes no sense. They hate sports and anything that takes physical effort. They love the chess club and the debating club — and politics, being Young Liberals. Who knew they would sign up? We were all so shocked. But it seems all the Jewish boys have signed up. They want to get rid of Hitler and fast — before he gets over here, maybe, and gets rid of us!

When they were sent over they had hardly been trained at all. If he has to fight, what will he do? I know I never *used* to worry, but this is different. Maybe I've just never had anything worth worrying over. Now I certainly do.

The trinket Morris sent me is a lovely, tiny little elephant made from wood. I've put it on my desk.

And oh yes, what he said about fifth columnists. Hah! I know all about that! The book I'm reading, *N or M?*, another Agatha Christie, is all about that. Fifth columnists might be all about in England, according to the book, but hopefully the secret police have discovered most of them. Still, I will keep my eyes and ears open right here. Spies can be anywhere!

DECEMBER 8

Dear Diary,

There's so much to tell these days that I hardly know where to begin. Got to school cold and miserable because I didn't eat my breakfast — I couldn't bear sitting at the table with Mommy, who looks as though she hasn't slept since Saturday. And every day the news gets worse, not better.

Thousands were killed at Pearl Harbor, thousands! The sailors were all just sitting on their ships and the Japanese bombed them and destroyed the ships and killed so many. The president is going to declare war, everyone says. And then when I got home for lunch, the paper read, CANADIAN UNITS AT HONG KONG IN WAR SECTOR. I know what that means without asking Mommy. It means Morris and Isaac and countless other Winnipegers. This morning when I got to school that's all anyone wanted to talk about, because it seems everyone in class has a brother or cousin or friend in the Grenadiers. Everyone was upset except, of course, Elizabeth. She has a cousin in the RCAF, but she's the oldest child in her family and her father is too old to go, so she's not too worried. But also, she refuses to be sad. She says it's our duty to be happy, or Hitler wins! So she won't hear of any worries or problems and just wants to have a good time. Whenever I worry or get sad Elizabeth sings, "Smile, though your heart is aching." I couldn't believe it when she first sang it because it's been my favourite song for ages. I have to admit that it does cheer me up.

What a difference between Elizabeth and Marcie. Marcie is the original Gloomy Gus.

But where was I? Oh yes, school. Mrs. Davis spent the first part of the morning explaining to us where the Grenadiers were — she showed us a map and then had each of us who have relatives there give a little speech about them. That was nice. I think we all felt better afterward, as if just thinking about them and talking about them could help in some way. I worry most about how frightened Morris must be, although I didn't say that in class. But he's a big baby, even though he's 6 feet tall and towers over chubby Isaac. And he's afraid of thunder and wasps and he hates mosquitoes — there must be a gazillion mosquitoes there, by the way.

Anyway, I suppose I was looking pretty glum at recess, so Elizabeth gave me a scathing look and then pulled my mouth into a smile. She organized a skipping competition and I must admit it did take my mind off everything. Especially since I won!

When I got home from school the final edition of the paper was sitting on the kitchen table, the headline: U.S. AND BRITAIN DECLARE WAR ON JAPS AS FIGHTING SPREADS. And of course the prime minister has declared that Canada is at war with Japan, so that's it; after two years, we're finally all in it together.

DECEMBER 9

It's late and I'm tired so this will be short. I went to ballet as I always do on Tuesday and then over to Marcie's for dinner. I took the streetcar to her house and then Mommy picked me up from there. I was almost relieved to be with Marcie after Elizabeth's non-stop cheerfulness. It was also nice to be back in the familiar north end. I guess the few months we've been in the south end just haven't been enough for me to feel as if I really belong. As soon as I got off the streetcar, it was like putting on an old pair of pyjamas.

Marcie, as usual, was full of gloom. But even that

was so predictable it was comforting.

"We may as well enjoy ourselves now," she said (which was pretty funny since she never does), "because when Hitler gets here we'll be the first to be rounded up and then . . . " At this point she made a motion with her hand of her throat being slit.

"Don't be a goose," I scolded her. "Hitler will never get to Canada."

"Then why," she said, "does the paper says the Pacific coast is 'on alert' and there might be black-outs? Oh, they're coming here. It's just a matter of time." I tried to get her off the morbid subject by asking about her brother. I tried not to blush when I mentioned Mark's name. I know she suspects I'm in love with him, but she's too good a friend to tease me about it.

She actually smiled for a change. They *had* heard from him. "He's not sure where he'll be sent next," she said. "He's still in England for the moment. They need doctors there right now because of all the flyers coming back injured." She stopped then and caught herself. "Sorry."

I sighed. "If Adam ever crashed his plane and needed a doctor I only hope it would be Mark," I said.

"Mark used to joke that the way they rushed him through medical school, it's a miracle he hasn't killed anyone yet. But he's able to go on leave to London and see the best theatre."

"I'd like to go with him," I said.

"You wouldn't like to be bombed every night," she said, shaking her head.

I corrected her and told her that the Blitz is pretty much over now. So she shot back that that was because Hitler was probably figuring out how to bomb us right here in Canada!

I told her about Sarah. Her response? "No doubt it's just a matter of time before Hitler finishes off everyone who's against him."

Honestly, by the time Mommy picked me up, I was wishing I had a friend who was not either all happy like Elizabeth or all sad like Marcie. I told that to Mommy, and she said that she and Daddy often used to say that about Adam and Morris — if only Adam could give Morris a little of his reckless spirit and Morris could give Adam a little of his caution. But it doesn't work that way.

Did I mention that I've finished *N or M?* and I'm now reading *The Man in the Brown Suit*, also by Agatha Christie? It's very exciting. Mommy has no idea I am reading it. There are some very racy parts, but I took it out of the library and told the librarian it was for Mommy. I read it at night when I'm supposed to be sleeping. There is quite a bit of passionate kissing and even talk of how Anne cannot stay too long with her *amour* or he might forget himself! I'm pretty sure I know what that means, but not completely sure, and there is no one to ask without admitting that I'm reading it.

I said this would be a short entry and now I've rambled on and I do want to finish the book tonight. So, more tomorrow!

DECEMBER 11

The U.S. has now declared war on Germany and Italy. And the paper says that the Hong Kong troops have beat back the Japanese. Two boatloads of Japanese were sunk. That must be a good thing.

Chanukah will be here soon. Usually it's all I dwell on for weeks ahead, but this year I hardly wanted to think about it. Without Adam and Morris here what fun will it be? But there was a party at the synagogue so we all went. I ate latkes and chocolate Chanukah gelt and played lots of games — mostly different dreidel games. Many of my friends from Aberdeen School were there, including Marcie. We were so excited to see each other and the girls loved my dress — a purple velvet dress I was sent from our cousins in New York. (By the way, Mommy says that there were two air-raid warnings in N.Y. the other day.

Wonder if that will happen here anytime soon?) But back to the dress — there were even white stockings to go with it. Mommy put my hair up in a curly mass and I could see Mordechai looking at me with a nice look that said he thought I was not too bad! I never see him now we've moved but I think he still has a crush on me.

Hester was there too, and as usual she couldn't stop talking, about how wonderful everything in the south end is, so much better than the north end, so much fancier, better schools, better shops, better everything. Naturally that didn't go over too well with my Aberdeen friends. I don't want them to think I'm a snob just because she is! They were glaring away at her as she was talking but she didn't seem to notice.

When we got home Mommy and Daddy gave me a brand new pair of skates for a present! They are so beautiful. White as snow.

I feel a little sick. I've eaten way too many latkes.

DECEMBER 12

I had completely forgotten that I had promised to have three squares knitted by today. Last night, after the party and after I'd written in my diary I suddenly remembered. I knitted till my fingers were ready to fall off. I did get the three squares done, even though

I was plenty bleary-eyed this morning! My class now has enough to make an entire quilt. Mrs. Davis is very proud of us. She had us sing "Rule Britannia" after "God Save the King," and then told us that we were a ripping good crowd! And then we all did three "hip hip hoorahs." I love having a British teacher. Her accent, for one thing. It's so, well, sophisticated. Even when she says the most ordinary thing it sounds smart coming from her. And she says we must have a "never say die" attitude. Very much like Elizabeth.

Oh, and I must report that Hedda Hopper has had very little of interest to report in her column recently. I was hoping for some juicy gossip to take my mind off things, but it is just a bunch of boring news. Spencer Tracy has passed up a Broadway show to do another movie. That's hardly earth-shaking.

Before I go to sleep I always pray to God to keep everyone safe. I start with *Dear God, please keep* . . . and then I list all the names, just the way Mommy taught me. The last few nights I've put in a special prayer for Morris and Isaac. I hope God listens, but I have my doubts.

LATER

Just as I'd finished writing, Daddy came to tuck me in. So I asked him if he thought God listened to our prayers.

"Uh, oh!" he said. "Another big question. I can tell by the tone of your voice."

"I'm praying for Morris and Isaac," I explained. "But why should God choose Morris to save over someone else? Wouldn't that be mean?"

"Morris is better than anyone else," Daddy said.

"Well, you know that and I know that but I'll bet all families feel that way," I answered.

"Of course they do," Daddy agreed. "I was trying to make a little joke." He paused and thought for a moment. "You know that quilt you are making at school? Each child makes a square, correct?"

"Yes," I said.

"And none of you knows what the other squares will look like. Perhaps that is the way God works. We are each like one of the squares. We choose how our own square will look, we choose the colour, the design, all of that. But when we are put in with the other squares we might be in the middle, at the edge, make the whole look one way or another . . . And it's when we interact with all the other squares that the unexpected can happen. And it can change the way

21

our square is viewed." I must have looked puzzled. "It's a mixture of our choices and God's choices. And it all makes a pattern, but only God can see the big pattern." He patted my hand. "I can't give you a simple answer, Devvy. Life is complicated and so is God, I think."

"So we can't be sure, can we," I said, "that Morris will be all right just because he's good. Because good people die, don't they?"

"Good people are dying every day," Daddy sighed. "Everyone who fights Hitler is a good person dying."

I started to cry. "It isn't fair."

Daddy hugged me. "It's life," he said. And I think he cried a little too, although he didn't want me to see.

"Now," he said, "I have a new joke."

Daddy has a theory that when people are laughing they don't feel pain as much, so he always tells jokes as he drills their teeth. Here's how this one goes:

"Your tooth is abscessed," the dentist said to Mr. Jones. "I'm afraid I'll have to pull it."

"H–how much will it cost?"

"One hundred dollars. But no choice, it must come out."

"A hundred dollars? That seems like an awful lot for two minutes of work."

The dentist shrugged. "If you'd like, I can pull it very, very slowly."

I giggled despite myself, so of course Daddy had to tell me another one:

"Why don't dentists eat much?"

"Why?" I asked.

"Because most of what they do is filling."

I hit him on the shoulder and said I hoped he didn't tell his patients that one. It's terrible. He assured me that they laugh anyway and then he told me not to stay up too late with my diary and my reading.

I thought about what he said after he left, and decided that I'd best keep praying for Morris and Adam and Isaac and Mark. Well, I'll just ask God to keep all our family and friends and everyone over there safe. After all, it can't hurt, right?

And of course I said special prayers for Sarah and her family, just like I do every night.

I just wish I were old enough to fight. And not a girl! After all, I'm named after a great fighter. I'd sign up and go kick Nazis all the way to Timbuktu!

DECEMBER 13

We stood in line for a sneak preview today at the Uptown, and it turned out to be *The Great Dictator*. Oh my gosh, dear diary, you have no idea how funny it was!! I was holding my stomach I was laughing so hard and I even dropped all my popcorn on the floor.

Elizabeth almost threw up she laughed so hard — she got the hiccups and couldn't stop. Dictator Hynkel fights the Jews and Napaloni, Dictator of Bacteria!! *Bacteria.* I'm laughing still, just thinking about it.

By the way, I've decided to make a list of people I like from class and people I don't. Guess what Mary said today when we were playing around the new building site down the street. "I hope no more Jews are going to move in here." And this just after seeing the Chaplin movie. She's part of the group of girls that I seem to be stuck with. I miss all my Jewish friends from the north end, that's for sure. I realize now what a swell bunch they are — now that I'm not there anymore. So I said, "I'm Jewish." And she said, "Well, I knew that." As if that was different somehow or didn't matter or what she said was not mean. I can just hear her parents saying it and her repeating it. They are such snobs. And no one said anything to her, not even Elizabeth.

So I'm making a list of nice and not nice. N stands for nice. S stands for snob. G for part of our group that plays together after school.

Girls:
Alexandra — N, G, shorter than me
Sandy — N, G, freckles all over her!
Mira — N, G, very skinny
Leslie — N, G, quiet

Elizabeth — N, G, very smart, always happy
Mary — S, G, also very smart
Jane — N, best skipper at school
Sandra B — S, enough said!
Francis — goof
Hester — G, Jewish, nice but talks non-stop, hence annoying
Devorah — perfect! Maybe a little short, skinny, long dark hair (way too curly), brown eyes.
Boys:
Peter — N, G, smart
Marvin — N, cute
Allan — N, almost as tall as me. In other words, a shrimp.
Paul — N and lives on my street, G, also cute, freckles, red hair, big smile, shy, seems to like me
Maury — S
John — N, and smart
Joshua — Jewish and cute, black curly hair
Terry — N
Robert — crazy — would be funny if he married Hester. Imagine the children they'd have!

I wanted to talk to Mommy or Daddy about Mary's remark, but they were huddled over the newspaper. I saw the headline: JAPS CLAIM CITY OF KOWLOON TAKEN.

"Isn't that where Morris was?" I asked.

"Yes," Mommy answered, "but they all moved from there, according to the papers. And it says here that where they are is a secret." I guess they have to keep it secret — they don't want to tell the enemy, do they?

Then she said she'd made my favourite for dinner. I tried to look excited. My favourite used to be cabbage rolls. No one makes them better than Mommy. But she forgets that since the boys aren't here she never makes *their* favourites — she makes *mine* all the time. Cabbage rolls could turn out to be my most hated meal.

Mommy has been out at Hadassah meetings all week, with no time to cook. They are planning a huge tea to raise money for Palestine, and another event, a fashion show, to raise money for the troops. Mommy looks a little better. I guess keeping busy has helped take her mind off what's happening in Hong Kong. (And saved me from cabbage rolls.)

DECEMBER 14

We spent the afternoon over at Auntie Adele's. The river is frozen deep so we went tobogganing and then had the usual feast — chicken soup and chicken and *shmaltz* and herring and that chocolate cake she makes and her homemade doughnuts and oh yes her pickles. The adults talked about the boys and how they might be doing and Baba Tema sat there looking stern, as if we were all criminals. She scares me. I must admit to you and you only, diary, that not seeing her every single Sunday since we've moved to the south end is hunky-dory with me. She never talks to me and I always think that she's sitting there thinking what a stupid mug I am. Course she doesn't talk much to anyone. Daddy is not at all like her, thank goodness. He talks all the time and tells jokes and never, ever makes me feel stupid — just the opposite. I'm sure I'm not as smart as he thinks I am. Well, maybe I am, I can only hope! Cousin Jenny let me try on some of her clothes and hats, even though they were all too big for me. She's almost sixteen, and she's so pretty. She can play piano like an angel. She goes over to the child-minding centre on Stella and plays piano for the children who have to stay there all day because their mothers are working in the factories now. Everyone plays piano, except me, because I refused to practise. It was so boring! I'm sort of sorry now though, especially when I hear her play. Uncle Simon did magic tricks after dinner. I wish he could make this whole war and Hitler and the Nazis disappear. Wouldn't that be perfect?

DECEMBER 15

Did I mention that I've put a map up on my wall? They had it in the Saturday *Tribune*. Now I can see where Morris might be when the stories come out about the Grenadiers in Hong Kong. Kowloon is right there on the mainland across from the island of Hong Kong.

I don't think I did very well in the math test today. I can't say I bothered to study. Who cares, after all? Don't I have enough to worry about? Still, Morris will be very unhappy if I let my schooling go. He wouldn't want me to use him as an excuse not to do my work. So I'd better study for the history test this Friday.

Meanwhile, at dinner Mommy wondered if she'd be called up to work in the factories or for the war effort in some way, because today in the paper it was announced that there's going to be a mobilization of both men and women for the war effort, with no exemptions. But the hardest thing to see in the paper today was a picture of the Canadian troops in Hong Kong. We got out the magnifying glass and tried to see if we could pick out Morris or any of the others we know, but no luck. And then the paper said that the troops were withdrawing from the mainland and moving to defend the island of Hong Kong. So far, only two Canadians reported wounded from the battle in Hong Kong and neither of them Morris. So maybe it's not so bad as I imagined.

After dinner we all listened to the news on the radio and then we listened to *The Lone Ranger*. That was fun and for a while it all seemed normal except not really because Adam isn't here acting out all the parts as the story happens, and Morris isn't here complaining that the radio is too noisy and he can't study. I miss them both so much.

DECEMBER 16

A letter just for me from Adam!! Here it is.

Dorset,
December 1, '41

Dearest Dev,
   I've been skating! Yes, they actually have rinks here and I took a fresh young English Rose, named Emily, and taught her how. It was fun and I was considered quite the gent when she fell and I carried her all the way to the pub! Some of the fellows are using their time off to play small pranks — that same night, they got a very friendly dog quite drunk.
   We like it down here on the southern coast, and I'm glad to report that so far we've only lost two from

my team. Remember Billy Lawson? He got so fearful of going back up he just couldn't do it and he was branded a coward and then they found he'd hanged himself behind the barracks.

Don't tell Mom and Dad this — remember our pact. Since you never worry, I tell you the truth of it and them the pretty version.

I take the little bear you gave me with me on every flight and so far he's done a good job of keeping me safe. And it's funny, isn't it — you couldn't have known that our squadron would be called the Winnipeg Bears. A grizzly, our badge, is supposed to represent courage to the Indians — whenever I need a little extra I just give Winnie a small squeeze and it helps.

Give my love to everyone and thank Moms for the Laura Secord chocolates. They were delicious. And the scarf she knit just fits the bill! I could use some extra warm winter undies — my gosh it can get cold here. It's the damp that seems to get into your very bones.

Cheerio!!

Love,
Adam

Adam is starting to sound almost as British as the king! Must remember to tease him about it in my next letter.

I guess it's not so long ago when I didn't worry

about anything. I worry all the time now. But I guess Adam needs to tell someone what is really going on and he just can't bring himself to tell Mommy. Daddy would be OK. He's always calm. And Mommy isn't what I would call a worrier — she just gets so mad, you don't want to get her started. For instance, when we catch a cold we need to brace for a big angry lecture about not wearing our hats or boots and it's our fault and if we get pneumonia and die it'll be our own fault and on and on. He'd better not get hurt, that's all I can say.

LATER

I was so excited about my letter from Adam I almost forgot Morris, until I got the bad news at dinner — the island of Hong Kong might have to be evacuated!! Daddy isn't sure they'll be able to do it, though. He's worried that they waited too long.

We practised for our dance recital today at ballet. I can forget all the bad news there and just concentrate on my dancing. Mommy has sewn me a lovely butterfly costume with yellow wings made from an old dress. I'm getting a little nervous — the concert is only a week away!

Mommy had a fit when I told her about Adam's request for more underwear. She was so upset that he didn't have absolutely everything he needed she could barely wait for tomorrow for the shops and the post office to open. He'll have that underwear so fast he won't believe it. She says this time she's including gum and hard candy. And four extra pairs of wool socks, just in case.

DECEMBER 20

We have two airmen here this weekend from the air training station at Gimli. Mommy finds out who the Jewish boys are from her Hadassah group, and invites them for Shabbat. They stay for a couple days and get well fed and seem to appreciate it. These two are very nice, a British fellow, George, and a Canadian from B.C., Larry. They each have their own room and they go out after dinner to dances, just like so many others on leave. There are lots of young women who make sure to go to these dances. Very patriotic of them, the boys say.

Flyers seem to be a happy bunch. They always joke around and have fun. Adam certainly is like that.

DECEMBER 22

The Japanese claim they have taken over 700 prisoners, most of them Canadians. Our paper says we're still fighting and holding them off, but this other news comes from German radio. Mommy insists it's all propaganda and we shouldn't believe a word of it.

I'm sorry I haven't written for a bit but I've been so busy practising for the recital tomorrow. We are terribly worried about Morris. We listen to the radio every night and read every scrap in the newspapers but so far nothing except they are still fighting. Auntie Adele is almost crazy with worry about Isaac. She can't stand to think about him and Morris fighting because they don't know how, number 1, and number 2, they wouldn't want to hurt anyone! I just hope they get over that and kill anyone they need to in order to stay alive.

Yesterday morning I spent at Marcie's. She and I discussed books like we always do. I just started a new Agatha Christie but there's a part right at the beginning that makes me feel strange. She describes a Jew and how he knows all about money. Suddenly I wondered if Agatha Christie hates Jews too, like everyone seems to these days. I felt like crying because she's my favourite author right now. I wonder if I should stop reading her. I asked Marcie what she thought.

She said something odd. "Everyone thinks about Jews like that," she said, "so why bother about it? I mean, if you like reading her, just ignore that part. Why should you suffer because she's stupid like that and then you can't read her and you like to?"

I wondered if I shouldn't take a stand and refuse to have anything to do with her. But Marcie thought not, because Mrs. Christie would never know whether I was reading her and therefore it wouldn't change her mind one way or another. Then I had an idea — I'd write her. Because maybe she doesn't even realize that she is hurting people's feelings.

We spent the afternoon writing a letter to her and then we put a stamp on it and I mailed it today! Here's what I wrote — more or less.

Dear Mrs. Christie,

I am one of your biggest fans. I love your books, even though my parents don't always know I read them. I am Jewish. In And Then There Were None *you write about a Jew and how he knows all about money. Some Jews do, but I need to tell you that Jews don't know any more about money than anyone else. We're just like anyone else. Some of us are good and some of us aren't and some are smart and some aren't. I like to dance and read and I don't think I'm different from the others in my class who aren't Jewish — I'm just different because I'm me. So I hope you will write your books with that in mind from now on and then I can read them without feeling sad.*

Your biggest fan,
Devorah Bernstein

I hope she answers me. In the meantime I may as well finish the book because it is already very exciting. It is set on an island and all these people with strange pasts have been invited to the island, but we don't know who's behind the invitations, and then one by one the people start to die! Well, of course, it *is* a murder mystery!

Around three o'clock we went over to the Hebrew Sick Benefit Hall and met up with Mommy and Daddy there, before going to Auntie Adele's. There was a Chanukah tea to raise money for children in Palestine. And some of those children are the lucky ones who have escaped Hitler. I got a teacup reading. It was spooky what the woman said — that I had three people I was worried about and that I should keep them in my prayers. And that I loved to dance. And that one day I would make a difference in the world! How could she know all that? I wish she knew if Morris and Adam would be safe. And if Sarah will get safely over here to Canada with her whole family. But the woman said there are too many people in trouble now for her to get a clear reading on anyone in particular. So I said, "What about Hitler?" And she said, "Good always defeats evil in the end. But how many will have to die first? More than we can imagine, I'm afraid." That gave me chills down my spine. Chills.

Wish me luck for the recital tomorrow.

December 23

The recital went as well as it could have. I didn't make a mistake and I think I danced at the top of my form and so did everyone else. Poor Sylvia fell over while doing a pirouette, but she got up again right away. She cried after, but we all joked around pretending to fall over too, and pretty soon she was laughing. And then we all went out for Chinese food at the Nan King. What a great night!

December 24

The paper today: HONG KONG TROOPS HIT BACK; CANADA WOUNDED BEING TREATED SATISFACTORILY. So they maybe still have a chance to win. And at least the wounded are being cared for. I'm hopeful.

December 25

The news on the radio tonight is very upsetting. Rumours that Hong Kong has fallen. Since it's Christmas Day we were going out for Chinese food with the whole family like we always do, but then Mommy wanted to stay home and listen to the news. So only Daddy and I went, and when we came home Mommy wouldn't say much about what she heard on the radio.

DECEMBER 26

Morris's picture was in the paper today. But I can hardly bear to write this down. The headline: HONG KONG'S HEROIC DEFENSE ENDED.

And the earlier edition: FATE OF GALLANT GRENADIERS MARS CHRISTMAS FESTIVAL. ALL OF MANITOBA PLUNGED IN GLOOM BY FAR EAST NEWS.

Mommy is on a rampage. Why did the boys have to sign up? It's all Isaac's fault. He goaded Morris into it. (Actually I think it was the other way around.) And then to see his picture in the paper as one who has served. It made me proud. And mad. And sad. And terribly worried. They've surrendered. What will happen to them? When will the army tell us if he is all right? Will they even know so they can tell us? The paper says they fear casualties are heavy. And that the military will do everything they can to find out about the wounded. There are pictures too, which makes it all too real. And the paper says that they fought overwhelming odds and that at the end they'd run out of water.

In the same paper it says that the French are now making planes for the Nazis. So while they aren't busy sending Jews away they are busy helping the Nazis. I hate them. I need to write Sarah again, but I'm too upset right now.

If only we knew whether Morris is all right. I don't want him to be a prisoner, but at least that would mean that he's alive.

Mommy and Daddy were so upset they didn't know what to do with themselves. I insisted they take me to a movie. It probably seemed heartless to them, but there was no use sitting around crying all day. I needed to get them out of the house. *Dumbo* had just opened at the Met. After constant nagging they finally gave in. So we went and it was packed — we barely got in. I loved it. This adorable baby elephant who wants to fly. But you can never get away from the war. There was a documentary on about flyers and of course that just reminded us that we need to worry about Adam as well as Morris! Still, I think it helped to get out of the house and I even heard Mommy laugh a couple times. Then we went to The White House for ribs and that would make anyone feel better!

I don't have ballet tomorrow as we're off for the Christmas holidays and no school all week.

DECEMBER 27

Today Elizabeth, Sandy, Leslie and me went to Snell's Drug Store for lunch. We had our favourite, ham sandwiches with lots of butter on white bread with chocolate milkshakes. We've never kept kosher at home, and for some reason we can have bacon but not ham or pork of any other kind. Daddy says it's "kosher" bacon. Hester isn't allowed to eat at our house because of that but that's OK because she is so irritating. I never tell Mommy that I eat ham when I'm out, but we eat ribs — and they're ham. It makes no sense to me so I ignore it. Boy, it was delicious. And then we went to the Sat. afternoon special matinee, *Haunted Gold* with John Wayne. And there were cartoons — three of them! I ate three bags of popcorn and then came home and had the worst stomach ache. Mommy put me to bed with a hot water bottle and lots of scolding. Daddy came in to cheer me up and told me some more jokes:

A woman told her doctor that she kept thinking she was a refrigerator.

"I see," he said. "Does this disturb you?"

"Not really."

"Then I wouldn't worry about it," he said.

"But Doctor, I sleep with my mouth open."

"So?"

"The light keeps my husband awake."

I stopped Daddy from leaving then with a question. "Do you think Morris will be okay?"

"Morris isn't the strongest of them all, but he's probably the smartest of them all, and maybe that and a little luck will keep him going."

"Luck," I repeated. "What's luck?"

Daddy shook his head. "That's another big question."

"Is luck God deciding what will happen to us?"

"Maybe luck is just that — luck. Chance."

"At the Chanukah fair, the teacup reader told me lots of things she saw in my future. If she can see the future, maybe it's all decided and we're just playing our parts, like me being the butterfly in the dance."

"Or maybe nothing is decided and it's just chance what kind of breaks we get."

"Morris decided to get into the war — that wasn't chance."

"No," Daddy answered, "and there's one thing we can be sure of. What we decide *does* matter. Look at the Germans. They elected Hitler. Elected him! They love him! They line up in the streets for him. And the French? They don't have to help the Nazis the way they are. Help? From what your Auntie Aimée writes, the French officials are pushing the Nazis to send the Jews away. So maybe we shouldn't worry about fate and luck. Maybe we should just worry about what we *can* do, the choices we can make. One person can make a difference, Devvy, don't ever forget that. And never forget that your brothers decided to stand up against this tyrant and fight him. I'm proud of them. Mommy is too. She doesn't let on — I know she talks like she's mad at them. But down deep she knows they did right. Should they have waited for some other young person to do it for us? Should they have shirked their chance to make a difference?"

That got me thinking. "But what am *I* doing to help?" I asked. "I should be doing more."

"That's up to you, Devvy," he said. "I haven't told the boys what to do and I won't tell you, either."

As he got up to go downstairs he added, "The Red Cross is trying to find out the names of those who have been captured, remember. Hopefully we'll hear something soon." He kissed me goodnight. Then Mommy came in. I asked her if she was proud of the boys for joining up.

She made a face and then sat down on my bed. She sighed before she answered.

"I am proud of them no matter what they do," she said finally. "I'm proud because they are good boys and that means more to me than anything."

"Then why are you mad?"

"I suppose because I'm frightened," she answered, "if truth be told. And that makes me angry. And part of me thinks they could have stayed home and contributed here."

This is the first time Mommy has ever talked to me

this way. Daddy always does, as if I'm grown up and can understand. Maybe with both boys gone she's figuring that I'm more grown up than she thought. I am eleven after all, and in grade six. Next year I'll be in junior high!

I asked her then if it would be all right with her if I had a tea here at the end of next week to raise money for the Red Cross. I suggested we could have it in the sunroom. She thought that was an excellent idea, but warned me she'd be very busy all week with her Hadassah work, so she wouldn't be able to help me. But then she added that at least it would keep me busy. "That's not why I'm doing it!" I said, insulted.

So dear diary, that's the project for the week. I'll need to make a list of things I need to do and people to invite.

And Then There Were None is really gruesome, by the way. People are dying right, left and centre! I think I'm going to reread *Anne of Green Gables*. I need a break from all this blood and gore.

December 31

Well, it's New Year's and I need to make a resolution. I've thought a lot about it and so I want to vow to:

1: Try to get Sarah out of France
2: Eat less popcorn
3: Make a difference
4: Keep my room clean
5: Study more

Mommy and Daddy let me have friends over tonight and they had friends over too. Daddy said we shouldn't just sit in the dark and be depressed. So I invited Marcie and Elizabeth for a sleepover. I was a little worried about how they would get on together but it was never a problem. It was a high-spirited party. We sang songs around the piano and the grown-ups danced. Daddy made a little speech and said he hoped that by next year Canada would prove what a wonderful nation it is, by not only fighting the Nazis, but by allowing desperate people to flee those Nazis and come and live here with us. He gave me a little wink and I felt better, imagining Sarah right here next year, celebrating the New Year with us.

But since my friends are still here, I'll write more tomorrow!

It was sad when we all sang "Auld Lang Syne," though. I don't think there was a dry eye — probably in the whole city!

1942

January 1

Daddy took me and my friends roller skating today. We had fun but I had a hard time getting over the worry — the first lists came out from Hong Kong. There is one Grenadier listed as missing and eleven Canadians listed as wounded, but Morris wasn't on the list. So we wait.

Well, actually, diary, here's the rub. I didn't really have trouble getting over my worry — we had a fabulous time, all the more so since Paul was there with Terry and Josh. Have I told you how cute Paul is? He has freckles all over his face and bright red hair and a big smile. He's a bit shy, but I like that. The six of us skated together and I think Josh and Marcie hit it off and Elizabeth and Terry, even though Elizabeth says she likes Marvin more. We had loads of fun and I forgot about everything else and then when I got home I felt guilty. Mommy had spent the day writing letters to every MP she could think of, as well as the prime minister. She wants answers about what has happened to the Canadians in Hong Kong and she wants answers now.

The paper says that there was a grand New Year's

celebration in London last night. I wonder if Adam was there. They said that 3000 people were in Piccadilly Circus for midnight, singing "Auld Lang Syne" just as we did.

Oh, and I forgot to write that Winston Churchill is right here in Canada and he says that the soldiers in Hong Kong gave them precious days to defend the Far East. I'm cutting that out of the paper for Morris — so he'll see when he gets home how everyone was thinking about him and the others there.

JANUARY 4

I had my tea today. We had fun and it all went almost like clockwork. The girls came over at 9 this morning and we made peanut butter sandwiches, pickle sandwiches and tomato sandwiches. We baked peanut butter cookies — see the theme? — and also I bought penny candies at the drugstore. Almost my entire class came as well as my class from Aberdeen. They kept apart as if they were two teams. But I charged everyone a dime to come and so we made quite a lot of money, which I will donate to the Red Cross. Am too tired to write any more — but am going to sleep happy. Tomorrow back to school.

❈

January 6

Today was the coldest day of the year so far, -33! The walk to school felt like being out in a great big freezer, except it was a windy freezer. I couldn't believe all the secretaries and others waiting for the streetcar in their little hats and chiffon hose and high heels. When I'm grown up I'll wear a big parka and moccasins to work. Yeesh. I wore my toque and big scarf and boots and warmest coat and I was still frozen by the time I got to school. And then I had to wait for the streetcar for ballet after school and that was no fun at all. I walked over to the Curry Bldg. after class though and Daddy drove me home. But first as a special treat he took me to The Chocolate Shop for hot chocolate. Mmmm, that was good. At school Mrs. Davis told us that a Winnipeg pilot had done some heavy damage to two German supply ships. We were all very excited. And the pilot and his crew returned to base safely, too. She also discussed President Roosevelt's war plans and read to us from his latest speech. He said that just like the people in London, "We can take it. And what's more we can give it back ." All the kids in class clapped as she read.

January 9

A letter arrived from Sarah, again tucked in with mail from Uncle Nathaniel. Daddy says he must have a person who smuggles these letters out for him regularly. And that we're lucky he does.

Chère Devorah,

Our worst fears came to pass. It was the middle of the night on the 12 of December and we were woken from our sleep. Three huge bangs on the door. Scared me to death. I crept to my door and peered down the hall, too frightened to move. And then I heard the sound one most dreads here, someone speaking in German — well, not speaking, shouting. Maman ran to my room and told me to keep the door closed and not to come out. She told Rachel the same. And within minutes, she came to my door and sank down on my bed weeping. "They've taken him," she said. "Where?" Rachel asked, coming in. "To Drancy. Arrested."

And only days later the Germans executed 95 hostages and 53 were Jews. We didn't know if Papa had been one of them; we could get no news. Then one day a week later, he suddenly appeared. They'd released him. He refuses to say anything about what happened to him. He says almost nothing. He sits

and stares at the trees on the boulevard, bare of
leaves, forlorn and dreary.

I can hardly sleep anymore. I keep hearing that
sound over and over. The pounding on the door.
Sometimes I feel the sound will explode in my brain.

Chère Devorah, what is wrong with the world? I
don't understand any of this. Do you?

Your loving cousin,
Sarah

The letter from Uncle Nathaniel told of being arrested, but little else, except another question about how the visas are going. I can hear Mommy pacing back and forth downstairs right now, her voice raised, probably railing to Daddy about our government and why they won't let our family join us.

JANUARY 10

Walt Disney has made a Mickey Mouse gas mask. Am I the only one who thinks that's a bit odd?

JANUARY 11

I made up a parcel especially for Sarah today. I shopped for it yesterday at Woolworth's after ballet and then lugged it all home on the streetcar. I bought her a scarf and a blouse and a little charm bracelet. I know they aren't useful but I'm hoping they will cheer her up. I also bought bubble gum and lemon drops. I'm wrapping each item in this really pretty paper and then putting it all in a box and addressing it just to her. I hope it helps just a little. Mommy said she would mail it tomorrow when she mails Adam's package — she mails him one once a week like clockwork. I bought Adam his favourite Juicy Fruit gum and those huge gumballs he loves as well. (Mommy mails the packages to Sarah's family to an address in Spain and then someone manages to get it to the family. At least we hope it gets through, and that it isn't too dangerous!)

JANUARY 15

I'm sorry I haven't written the last few days but I've been so busy every night. Either I'm sat by the radio listening to our favourite shows and knitting squares for school, or me and the girls are out skating on the new rink the city flooded right over near Elm Street and Robert H. Smith School. It's a fabulous rink and we've been there almost every night. There's a shack to change your boots in and everything. Oh, here's a funny story. Paul was skating there two nights ago and someone took his boots. Well, he has new skates, just like me, and he didn't want to ruin them by wearing them home, so he ran all the way in his stocking feet!

At supper tonight Mommy and Daddy were very upset. They have good friends in Vancouver, the Mishimas, and today it was announced that all Japanese are going to be sent out of the city!

"They are just as Canadian as we are," Mommy said. "It's so unfair! They're going to forbid them cameras and radios." She sighed. "No one could love this country more than they do."

January 17

Marcie and I met downtown this afternoon after my ballet class and went to see the new movie, *Sergeant York*. I hated it! All the papers say it is great, but Marcie and I thought it was really boring. It's all about this hick and how he's a great shot, and then he gets hit by lightning and gets religion and becomes a conscientious objector, and gets called up and serves anyway even though he doesn't believe in killing. It's the First World War and single-handed he captures a whole bunch of Germans. Well, I liked that part — that part was very amazing because it's from a true story. But the rest was too long and boring. And I ate way too much popcorn and had a stomach ache all night!

Mommy took the train to Toronto. She's involved with a national group that will help organize for the men in Hong Kong. They had their first meeting tonight. When she gets home she'll organize a Winnipeg chapter. They have registered with the Red Cross and are arranging food baskets and such. But still no news of the fate of the men who were captured. Mommy has been much better though since she got busy with this. And I've been extra busy looking after Daddy, although Martha has been staying later than usual whenever she comes to clean, and making dinner for us both. But I make his tea every night.

And in the paper today were the first pictures from the battle of Hong Kong. I look at them and wonder if Morris was right there.

Oh, and the last thing I need to report — Carole Lombard was killed in a plane crash! Along with her mother! She'd been on a trip to help sell defence bonds. Here's the part of the story that really bothers me. She was travelling with Clark Gable's publicist, who wanted to take the train. Carole wanted to fly. They tossed a coin and Carole won. They flew, and they died. What does that mean? Was it just chance that the coin fell the way it did? Is that how little our lives mean? Or was God behind it and was she meant to die that way? Or as Daddy says, is it somehow a combination of both things?

I know one thing — I don't understand it. Will Adam's survival, or Morris's, depend on something little like that? Like a toss of a coin? It makes me feel like everything must be terribly important, even the toss of a coin, or nothing is important, and we may as well not care about anything.

JANUARY 21

It's spring! It was 35 degrees today and the rinks got all slushy! So after dinner we listened to *The Thin Man*, then *The Shadow*, then *The Lone Ranger* and then *The Green Hornet*. A whole night of adventure! Of course, since I've been out skating every night I lost track of the stories and Daddy had to fill me in, although he only listens to *The Thin Man*, so we were a little behind but soon figured it all out.

Still no word from Hong Kong.

JANUARY 26

Mommy is back from her trip.

Today we had a letter from Auntie Aimée. She sounds low, and who can blame her? She pleads for Mommy and Daddy to help. Mommy got angry at the prime minister all over again and paced up and down, and ranted about how horrible the govern-ment is and how they are condemning our families to death! Daddy said she was exaggerating, and she said he'd heard what was going on there, and I asked what and she said never mind, but I asked again and she said that the Germans were taking people to camps and killing them. And Daddy said that was probably just a rumour and Mommy said that Auntie Aimée didn't think so and there was no use hiding it from me. And I agreed with her because I want to know the truth. And Sarah mentioned *rumours* but didn't say what they were. Surely they couldn't be killing Jews? Whole families? That couldn't be. Could it?

JANUARY 28

Am reading *Sad Cypress* at night, trying to take my mind off what Mommy told me is happening in France. There is a passage in the book where Poirot says that life is not reasonable. He's right, isn't he? He says life doesn't let you arrange and order. That's true too. If only we could demand some sort of, I don't know, reason or logic or something so things could make sense. Everything seems so out of order. And such bad things are happening. Does God want them to happen? Does He make them happen? Or does He just watch and feel sad? Why did He have to make a world where sad and cruel things happen all the time? Still, I must remember that there are so many good people, I mustn't let the bad ones ruin my life. But it's hard.

FEBRUARY 3

A strange and bizarre thing has happened. I was walking home from school, when a young kid threw what I assumed was a snowball at my back. I yelled at him and thought nothing of it until Elizabeth gasped in horror as I turned to go into my house. "Your coat!" she shouted at me. "Take it off."

We hurried into the house and I took it off and turned it around so I could see the back of it. There was a swastika on it! Really. I screamed, dropping it to the floor. Mommy came running in from the kitchen. I pointed to the coat. She picked it up, looked at it closely and said, "Where did that come from?" in a very quiet voice.

Elizabeth said that a boy hit me with something.

"But he couldn't have drawn this," I said. "He just hit me with a snowball and ran."

Mommy had bought me the coat at a factory on Main Street, only a couple of months ago. She looked inside and there it was — a swastika in red dye. She said that the snow or damp must have brought it out, but I didn't understand.

"Someone at that factory is a Nazi," she said. "Or

is playing a terrible joke on the customers. I'm phoning Mr. Berdinsky right now."

We heard her angry conversation and his obvious apology. She got off the phone and said, "He wants to get to the bottom of this." He's bringing a new coat over himself tonight and picking this one up.

February 4

Mr. Berdinsky called to say that he had discovered the culprit, a nasty fellow who hated Jews. He'd got the job at the factory just to make trouble — he wanted to display the swastika and if a Jew bought the coat, even better. Well, now the police are dealing with him.

It's one thing to think about Nazis in Europe — it's another to realize they are right here.

February 7

Still no news from Hong Kong. No letters from Adam. No letters from Sarah even though I've written her twice since I sent the package. Still, I suppose we have no way to know what gets through to Sarah. We can only hope she gets our letters and parcels. I write Adam every week too. I know he gets those.

The weather finally got cold again so I've been skating and knitting my squares, and listening to the radio and going to movies. The usual. I guess you could say I've been a little blue too. After Mommy told me about the Jews being killed, and then with the coat incident, I started to have nightmares about the Nazis coming to the house and breaking down the door and dragging me off and sending me away from Mommy and Daddy. I wake up screaming and Mommy or Daddy has to run in and calm me down. Hot chocolate in the kitchen seems to work well.

A very sad story in the paper today — Clark Gable might retire because he's so heartbroken since Carole Lombard died.

February 13

We celebrated Valentine's Day at school today and everyone loved the valentines I made — I cut them to look like Spitfires and they said, *Here's a valentine speeding right for you!* Elizabeth's were the best though — she pasted them on lacy paper doilies she cut out herself. Mrs. Davis gave each of us candy. Definitely took our minds off Friday the thirteenth!

February 14

Saw Mickey Rooney and Judy Garland in *Babes on Broadway*. What a swell movie. Judy is the best singer and dancer in the whole world. I know I've thought about being a singer or a dancer but maybe I'd be better off being a doctor — I'll never be able to sing like her. Girls *can* be doctors now, just like Daddy being the first Jewish dentist in Winnipeg. There are still quotas in the universities for Jews, but maybe by the time the war is over those will be taken away because people here won't want to be like the Germans and they'll want Jews to have equal rights. And I'm good at science and I don't faint at the sight of blood. I bet I could do it! Although I suppose I'll need to do better at school.

When I think about what I want to be I can't help thinking about Sarah, and wondering if she'll ever get a chance to follow her dreams. She won't if we don't win, I know that much.

Mordechai sent me a valentine in the mail, and so did Marcie. I also got an anonymous one! And Mommy and Daddy gave me a box of Laura Secord candy. I ate too many at once — of course!

FEBRUARY 16

60,000 British troops were taken prisoner in Singapore. I feel terrible for them.

Today our school took part in the new Victory Loan Campaign. We had a jumble sale and a bake sale — I baked oatmeal cookies with almost no sugar

— and we raised $100! At the legislature the guns fired twice, telling the city that the province had passed the $2,000,000 worth of war bonds so far.

February 18

A short note finally from Sarah!

Chère Devorah,

Your package was simply wonderful! I loved the clothes and wear the scarf every day. It makes me feel so special. And you remembered that blue is my favourite colour. Of course you would! The sweets were also perfectly delicious and this time Maman let me keep them — she didn't barter them away — and I shared them with Rachel. We have been eating a few every day and it makes the day seem so special. Just between you and me, if you send small amounts like that Maman doesn't seem to think they will really be useful to barter so I get to enjoy them. Your mother's packages go straight to the black market.

It is cold here but some days I smell spring in the air. Maybe with spring and flowers and sunshine the Germans will start to lose. That's what I imagine, that they will all wither in the light of the sun.

Hope you are well.

Your loving cousin,
Sarah

I want to send her packages as often as possible, but Mommy says that I can't. Every time we send a package someone puts himself in danger to deliver it. The packages are helping the family stay alive right now, so it's worth the risk, and Mommy says Uncle Nathaniel pays well for them, but it all has to be organized by Mommy from now on. Tomorrow there's going to be an "If Day." The province will act as if it's being invaded by the Nazis.

February 19

Because we're in grade six we were walked over to Robert H. Smith to take part in the If Day activities with the junior-high students. We were prepared for what would happen by Mrs. Davis, but I can tell you it was scary! We joined the rest of the students in the gym. The "Nazis" came in dressed in real uniforms, which Mrs. Davis said they rented from Hollywood. They arrested Mr. Bruce because he's the principal there, right in front of us all, and then announced that only the "truth" would be taught from now on. One of them called a kid up and measured his head. He said the student's head was the wrong measurement, which must mean he was a Jew and would have to leave the school.

Then they asked all other Jews to stand up, but we

didn't! I was ashamed and afraid and I just sat there and so did the others. Except Jonathan Chechensky from grade nine and he got up and screamed, "I'm Jewish and I'm not afraid of you!" And then he was led out. And then we were instructed that we must all swear loyalty to the Führer or be arrested. And we must all be spies — if anyone was not loyal we needed to turn them in. And all the books would be burned that the Germans didn't like, which would happen at a big bonfire. And we could only read what they approved of. Then the assembly was dismissed.

We walked back to our school. Once back in class Mrs. Davis led a discussion about how we felt. I felt mad. I was mad that I hadn't stood up to them. And it was only pretend! Mrs. Davis explained that it is very hard to fight people like that and what we felt was normal and that we needed to do all we could to help the war effort. But suddenly I wondered if everyone was looking at me differently because I'm Jewish. There are only a few of us in class, unlike at Aberdeen where practically the whole class is Jewish. And for the first time I wished that I was back there. Mrs. Davis was nice and told everyone that we could all be treated like that for various reasons — in Germany if you belonged to the wrong political party you could be arrested, for instance.

Still, I feel ashamed that I didn't stand up. I didn't tell Mommy or Daddy about it. It's my secret.

The papers today printed an edition pretending that the Nazis had taken over. Some of the "orders of the new government" say that no civilian will be permitted on the streets between 9:30 p.m. and daybreak, that all public places are out of bounds to civilians, and not more than eight persons can gather at one time at any place, and that every householder must provide accommodation for at least five soldiers.

The new "rules and regulations" go on and on — the Boy Scouts will be taken over by the Nazis and so will the Girl Guides, and everyone will have ration cards, and death without trial for attempting to organize resistance, or entering or leaving the province without permission, or failure to report all goods possessed, possession of firearms, etc. etc. etc.

Mayor Queen and Premier Bracken and his whole cabinet were "arrested." Pictures in the paper show them being led away by Nazis. Daddy came home and told me that his bus was stopped and searched. He said it gave him chills, realizing that if it had been real, he would have been taken away just for being a Jew.

Marcie called me and told me what happened at Aberdeen. Apparently Joe decided that they would resist when the Nazis arrived and he organized the entire school into resistance cells. They spent the day planning ways to secretly fight the Germans, how to hide Jews from them, and how to bring the Nazis down from within. They split into small cells of five or six, the way we've heard they work in France, and some students were "collaborators" who helped the Nazis. I wish I'd thought of that! Makes me look at Joe in a different way — he always seems so quiet to me. I don't ever think of him as a fighter. Some of the teachers played the Nazis and they had some of the "Resistance" arrested. Very dramatic and scary.

It was all to raise more money for the Victory Loan. And the newspaper says that Manitoba topped $11,000,000 on If Day.

I kept thinking about Sarah. This isn't pretend to her. I need to do something, I realize that now. But what?

February 20

I didn't stand up and I'll never do that again. So now I know what I need to do. I'm going to personally write a letter to the prime minister and ask him to let Sarah come here.

February 21

I sent a copy to the prime minister. And I copied it to paste it here so he can never say I didn't write him.

Devorah Bernstein
78 Waverly Street
Winnipeg, Manitoba

Dear Prime Minister,
Many people of the Jewish community have written and asked you to let people from France and Europe into Canada, but you have never said yes. I am writing to ask you again, because we had an "If Day" here in Winnipeg. I'm sure you read about it. It showed what it would be like if the Germans invaded us. My father is a dentist and he is a good citizen. I am a good student. I could be better, and I am trying. Both my brothers are fighting for our country. We are Jewish. My cousin in France is Jewish. Her name is Sarah. She is a very talented pianist and would be a wonderful addition to our country. Please let her come here. Please help her and all the Jewish people in France.

Sincerely yours,
Devorah Bernstein

February 25

The house has gone quiet. Mommy and Daddy don't talk.

In the paper today the first numbers out of Hong Kong: 296 dead, 1,985 taken prisoner.

February 28

I escaped to Elizabeth's on Friday and spent the weekend with her. I tried to put everything out of my mind. The talk at dinner was all about the Oscars. What a relief from my house. When they talk it's war, war, war, and the boys, and who can blame them? Anyway, *How Green Was My Valley* won the Academy Award. Gary Cooper won for *Sergeant York* and I guess he was pretty good but I wasn't hoping for him, I was hoping for Cary Grant. Joan Fontaine won for *Suspicion* and I never saw that because it was an adult film. And I wish Greer Garson had won because I think she's just perfect!

I went to ballet as usual and then Elizabeth and I went to see *How Green Was My Valley*. Oh we just loved it! Now *that* was a movie! Maureen O'Hara was a dream. We played ring-a-levio with the whole street on Saturday night after supper, except the cage was a Nazi prison and the escape was Canada. And then on Sunday we continued the game all afternoon.

March 2

Just as I was leaving for school the doorbell rang. It was a young man and he had a wire in his hand. "Bernstein?" he said. I nodded. He handed it to me. Heart thudding in my chest, I walked into the kitchen. Mommy took one look at my face and let out a little cry. She snatched the telegram from me and tore it open. She stared at the words for what seemed forever. Finally she spoke.

"Adam is missing," she said.

"Missing?" I repeated.

"He was part of a raid on enemy territory, and his plane was hit."

I just stood there. She stood there. Then I went to the phone and called Daddy's office. I told him the news. He said he'd cancel his morning and be right home and that I was to sit with Mommy until he got there. I put the kettle on and made Mommy sit down. I made some strong tea with sugar in it and then I called Auntie Adele. She said she was coming right over. I made Mommy sip the tea. She sat there, all quiet. When Daddy rushed in she broke down and cried. He kept telling her that Adam would be fine. "'Missing' means missing, nothing more," he said. "And if anyone can land a plane it's Adam and if anyone can trick the Nazis it's Adam." That made me feel better. I stayed home in the morning and after Auntie Adele had given me lunch I went back to school. That's when Elizabeth told me that Paul wasn't there because his family had just heard that Paul's brother had been killed in Hong Kong.

When I got home from school the paper had Adam's picture on the front page and a whole article about the attack. I felt so proud of him and yet so useless! If only I could go over there and rescue him.

MARCH 5

I spent the week trying to raise money for the Victory Loan — the deadline for the campaign is tomorrow. I went through all my old clothes and toys and took them to school and so did all my classmates and we sold them to the rest of the school today and raised fifty dollars! At least it kept me busy all week. Mommy did the same. She got very busy with her Hadassah group. They had a big fundraising week with a fashion show yesterday and a jumble sale today.

MARCH 6

The total for Victory Loans — over $60,000,000. Paul came back to school today. I didn't know what to say to him. Mrs. Davis told him that the whole class was sorry for his loss and because of his brother we would be free and never have to truly experience what happened on If Day. When Adam's picture was in the paper she said something like that to me — I'm not sure because as soon as she started to talk I started to cry and I got so embarrassed I didn't really hear it. Elizabeth keeps telling me to buck up and that he'll be fine. She's driving me slightly mad.

LATER

The paper had terrible news — two prisoners of war from the Grenadiers dead. Daddy says it's horrible, but it gives us reason to be much more sure that Morris and Isaac are alive — if they weren't we would have heard. And I think he meant it, he wasn't just saying it to make me feel better.

Another story at the bottom of page one. A fighter bomber crashed into the North Sea and the crew was rescued because Winkle, a carrier pigeon, managed to fly back to base. Her code number showed the plane she'd been in and the crew had managed a weak SOS, and between those two things they figured out where the plane crashed and picked the crew up from their dinghy! So maybe Adam will be rescued somehow.

March 14

I met Marcie at the Capitol today after ballet and we saw *Captains of the Clouds*. Cagney as a fighter — it was inspiring. And what was especially amazing was that it was all set in Canada and was about the RCAF and even had Billy Bishop, a war hero, playing himself. After the movie we went back to Marcie's house and I had dinner there, before Daddy picked me up.

Imagine Sarah not being able to do anything like that anymore. She can't even go to a movie or out for a hot chocolate or anything. I'd go crazy.

March 15

Middle of the night and I still can't sleep.

Adam is back in England!

The telegram arrived after supper. This time Daddy answered the door and read the wire before Mommy even knew it had come — she was in the basement looking for things she could give away for a Hadassah auction. I knew it was good news when Daddy grabbed my arms and whirled me around the room. Then he told me to go get Mommy. I did. And he read the telegram. "Have arrived safely in England. Stop. Letter to follow. Stop."

Daddy grinned. Mommy sat down hard. I jumped

up and down and yelled and yahooed. Daddy poured himself and Mommy a brandy. They don't drink very much, but they were both pale as ghosts.

I'm so happy. But then I started to worry all over again. What happens on his next flight?

MARCH 16

Another wire from Adam. He's been recommended for a medal! It's called a DFC, which Daddy says is the Distinguished Flying Cross.

MARCH 17

I was a big celebrity at school today after Elizabeth made sure everyone heard about Adam's medal. I am so proud of Adam. Mrs. Davis made a very nice speech congratulating me and our family. But I couldn't help but sneak a few looks at Paul, whose own brother died. He seems so sad and doesn't talk much at all anymore. And I realize that I could be in his shoes at any moment, with either Morris or Adam.

The rinks are melting and any day now I'm going to be able to take my boots off and wear shoes when I walk to school. Can't wait.

MARCH 18

A new letter from Sarah today. Again tucked into one from Uncle Nathaniel.

Ma chère Devorah,

We are so miserable here and all I can say to you, is please, please, please, try to get us out. I know you are my age and can probably do nothing, but I sometimes despair if all is left up to the adults. Papa refuses to admit anything could happen to us, so I must be the one to tell you the bad news — Cousin Marie and her family have been deported to a camp in the south. They have written us a letter and the conditions are deplorable. This, however, is the good news. My Uncle Leslie and his wife and two children have been taken and we fear it is to the camps in Germany or Poland and once there, no one hears from anyone again. I think they are being killed! Yes, I'll say what Papa refuses to say or believe! And Rachel agrees. I wish I could help her with her work but I am too young, apparently. But not too young to die. Why Papa was released after they rounded up most of the top Jewish leaders, I don't know. Doctors, professors, scientists, lawyers, writers — so many of these people were our friends. Perhaps Papa has paid for his safety. But how long will that last?

I know this is a morbid letter, but who else can I

speak to? Please write back and tell me every detail of
your life, because it makes me happy that there are
still Jews in the world who are happy and living a
good life. Especially since they are part of my family.

The package your dear Mama sent has been most
welcome — as usual we have used the chocolate to
barter for food. And the clothes are lovely. I wish I
had somewhere to wear them.

Sending you a big hug,
Sarah

I have to do something! But what? I've written the prime minister and had no reply. Well, maybe we need to make a fuss so someone notices. I have an idea. What if all my classmates went down to the legislature and all together asked to see the premier. Then he could talk to Ottawa for us, correct?

LATER

I told Mommy my idea and she was dead against it. She's been in touch with all the bigwigs at the Jewish organizations and they don't want anyone making a fuss. They say they are working behind the scenes and have been told that if there is a public outcry, nothing will happen. "But Jews are being killed!" I said to Mommy.

"We don't know that for sure," Mommy said. But we do, diary, we do! Sarah is right. The adults are afraid to do anything. Now I don't know what to do! I'm going to write Adam and ask him. He knows best.

One more thing. The paper today: JAP INVASION FLEET WRECKED.

Twenty-three ships were sunk by the Americans and the Australians! Take that! When I think about Morris being a prisoner of the Japanese, maybe sick — who knows? — it just upsets me so much.

MARCH 22

Elizabeth and I went to see *Ball of Fire* today starring Gary Cooper and Barbara Stanwyck. We were laughing so hard and we really had a goofy time on the streetcar on the way home, talking in slang at the top of our voices and raising eyebrows, which made us pretty slap-happy. It's all about this stuffy professor who is writing an article for an encyclopedia about slang so he gets mixed up with this dance hall smooch — Barbara S. — who teaches him slang and of course they fall in love but she's mixed up with a gangster. The doll, or dish, is all about the dough, moolah, bucks, and she thinks the mug is a jerk and he gives her the screamin' meemies. When we got home I greeted Mommy with, "'Hidy Ho, what's the fever, what's buzzin', cousin?" She gave me a strange look and then said she'd made a roast for dinner and I said, "Knock yourself out, it's okey-dokey with me. But I have to shove in the clutch and do some homework before we chow down." She realized that I'd been to the movies so she said that I was a goofy kid and I said she didn't know from nothing and was about to say something else when the phone rang — which was just as well because I was running out of cute talk.

MARCH 24

At dinner tonight Daddy told us that we have to use the car only when really necessary — like for a big shopping or to go to the north end. Tires are not going to be replaced once they wear out. Fortunately the car is only two years old and Daddy thinks the tires will last at least a few more years. They are rationing gas but it's not a problem for most people who just drive around town. And Daddy also says there is going to be some kind of conscription. The age will be from 21 to 30, up from 25.

March 27

No school today! The storms that started a couple of days ago are so bad that school was cancelled. Yesterday only half the class was there. I trudged through the drifts to Elizabeth's and we spent the day together. By around 4 p.m. Sandy, Mary, Hester, Paul and Allan were over as well. I tried to talk about what we could do to help in the war, but as usual, Elizabeth only wanted to play and have fun and she chided me for trying to make everyone miserable. I hardly want to be friends with her anymore but if I break up with her she'll turn the others against me, I know she will. I'm going to call Marcie tomorrow and see what she thinks.

March 28

I couldn't call Marcie, all the phones were dead today! The snowplows are even stuck and everything has come to a halt in the city. Elizabeth came over with the rest of the crowd, except for Hester, who has just come down with chicken pox. We played all day, mostly hide-and-seek in the house, and then Monopoly. Mommy made us sandwiches and it was a fun day. No more of those if I break off with my school friends. Hope I don't catch chicken pox from Hester, by the way.

LATER

Just before bed Daddy came into my room with a big smile and a big package for me. He'd been saving it for the weekend, he said, because he knew I wouldn't get any sleep once I saw it. And then when I opened it! The brand new Agatha Christie, not from the library, bought just for me! *The Moving Finger.* It's a Miss Marple, but she doesn't even come in till near the end. I can tell you that because I only have three more chapters. And, I'm glad to say, no antisemitic remarks from Agatha Christie, so I've decided to forgive her. What a good story. I'm glad that now I don't have to hide her books anymore. Mommy and Daddy must think I'm growing up — finally!

EVEN LATER

It's around one in the morning and I just finished the book! It was all about misdirection and even though she tells you that, she still managed to misdirect me. I wasn't even close. I thought it was everyone except who it turned out to be — the murderer, of course. How does she do it?

I've had so much fun this weekend. Maybe Elizabeth is right and I'm just being silly. I can't do anything, I can't help. What's the point of worrying?

MARCH 30

Dear diary, a letter from Adam! Here it is. Mommy wanted to keep it, but I convinced her it would be safer in my diary.

Dearest Family,

I'm going to tell you a little bit about my adventures. I must leave names and places out for obvious reasons. The censors might not let it through and one wouldn't want any important information to land in the wrong hands.

My plane got into trouble over the French coast. I bailed out into a forested area, but luckily missed the big trees and only hurt my leg — just a badly twisted ankle. I buried the parachute and using my pocket knife cut the tops off my boots so they didn't look military. And then a truck drove up! I realized I couldn't outrun it so I was prepared for the worst when the fellow called to me from the dirt road and waved me over. I didn't know at that point if I was going to my doom but I had little choice — I couldn't outrun him. So I hobbled over and he waved for me to get into the back and pulled the tarps over me. Only about a minute later I heard a German voice. My Yiddish is good enough that I could make out what he was saying, asking if the chap in the truck had seen a parachutist. He replied that he had and that "he's gone that way." And then the truck roared off.

We travelled for about a half an hour and then stopped at a farmhouse. There was already another chap there, an American. I was quizzed by a short stout fellow who needed to verify that I was the real deal and not a German plant. He asked me lots of questions. Here's the funny part. The American also asked questions, because my French is not that good, as you all know. And he asked me baseball questions to see if I was really a Canadian! I didn't know any of the answers and told him, "Ask me anything about hockey and I'll give you the answer." Finally they seemed to accept me and it was obvious we — me and the American — had been lucky. The French Resistance was going to help us!

We were put into a root cellar and none too soon because Germans came shortly after and searched the house. The family had put a big piece of furniture and a rug over the opening and we weren't discovered. A couple days later another airman joined us, a French Canadian from Montreal. Paul. That was very useful as he was able to do all the interpreting for us and would be able to speak fluently if we were questioned down the road. Speaking of which, it was only a day later when we were dressed as locals and put on a train to Paris.

*We met three more airmen on the train and we
all travelled together. The compartments are all
separate, not like on our trains, so once underway we
could relax and not worry about being checked. But
just before we reached Paris, the Resistance fighter we
were with checked the fake passes we'd been given
and they were of such bad quality he ripped them up
and told us we'd be better without any papers. So we
needed to get through security in Paris without any
papers. We pulled into the station at the same time
as an entire troop train of German soldiers.*

*But no one stopped us. And that's when I was met
by my new guide, and I think you might guess who
that was — Leah's sister. Imagine my shock!! Paul
and I spent a few hours at the apartment and then
were taken from apartment to apartment for the next
few days and then finally given a new identity card
and taken to the train station. The braveness of our
Resistance companions will not soon be forgotten.
We had no sooner walked into the station than a*
gendarme *stopped me and Paul. We showed our
cards and Paul spoke for both of us and we were
waved on. My heart was in my throat. Once in the
train I recognized those from my earlier group. And
our angel, the one I mentioned earlier, was there too.
Our seats were reserved but there were others sitting
in them. And Angel, as I shall call her, just marched*

over and shouted at them to give us our seats, as if we weren't all fugitives! And they did! We stopped at dawn and had to say goodbye to our angel and someone else took over. We travelled farther, went to another house, and at night went by truck, around 30 of us by then, to a forest, a beach, and then without telling too much more detail we were picked up by a British boat and taken home. In the forest we actually came across a German outpost, but they were so drunk we were able to walk right past them without being stopped. We had little choice, there was no way around because there was a stream on one side and a cliff on the other! That was a hair-raising moment as well.

And that, dear family, is my adventure. I am sure you are doing all you can to help all angels and their families. It is terrible in France. The Germans are such bullies and even riding a streetcar might get you killed if you are an average citizen. If you are Jewish, well, it is well known now that Jews are being killed outright. There is a new term, Judenfrei. I've been told that in Poland they are making entire towns and cities free of Jews. And that means they are taking Jews away and killing them.

Should anything happen to me I want you to know that I have no regrets. We must fight these devils and fight them with all we've got. We need to *sacrifice and I am happy to do so. What we fliers do almost seems easy when I see what the Resistance does every day in France. So Moms, I know you worry. And Dev, you never used to but from the sound of your letter, you are lately. My advice is not to worry, but to get busy doing what you can to help. I know, Moms, that you are already doing a lot. And Dad, you are too. And Dev, your tea and fundraising will help too.*

Did I mention that I've been promoted?

That's all from here. Your package arrived and was enjoyed by all.

Love,
Adam

As soon as we got to the part about Leah's sister, Daddy thought a moment and then exclaimed, "Rachel — Leah's sister in the Bible! Rachel is obviously in the Resistance, and thanks to her and others like her, Adam was saved. That must be what Sarah meant when she said she wished she could help her sister in her work, but was too young."

So there it is. Adam had given me the advice I was looking for. I must do something. It's no longer a question. But what? *That* is the question.

April 2

We had the first Seder tonight. Baba Tema still insists on skipping nothing in the service before we eat and we are always so hungry, but this time I snuck little bits of matzah when she wasn't looking. Daddy did the service as usual, reading it all in Hebrew. And I was allowed a little more wine in my water, compared to last year, so by the time we ate I was feeling a little giddy and kept giggling. Baba Tema kept glaring at me. I hid the *afikomen* from Daddy so well that he couldn't find it even though he looked everywhere and so he paid me an entire 50¢ for it! And since I'm still the youngest, I had to ask the four questions, AGAIN, but I did them without too many mistakes. And then after we ate she insisted we do the entire service after the meal too, when I was drooping in my chair and practically asleep, head on the table!

The headlines in the paper today — a big bombing raid on France and Germany by the RAF; 15 bombers are missing. But as far as we know Adam isn't flying cover for bombers. Still, he could have been flying in some other area, who knows? He says not to worry, but how can we help it?

No school tomorrow as it's Good Friday. I'm staying in the north end and am writing this at Marcie's house. I've told her my thoughts about wanting to do something for Sarah. We're going to meet with a bunch of my old classmates tomorrow to plan strategy. Elizabeth has organized a movie day for the south-end gang for Saturday, but I've said no. She wasn't too happy with me. She told me that I could bring my other friends, but I told her we had other plans. I'm going to stay here until Sunday.

April 5

I'm back home, and I had a good weekend. It's funny, because it was so different from last weekend which was so much fun. We spent this one talking endlessly and fighting about what to do and yet tonight I feel better inside than I did at the end of last weekend. It wasn't that I had fun, but I just feel we accomplished something, or at least we tried to do something to make things better and somehow that feels better than just trying to have fun and not worrying about anyone outside of yourself. Maybe there's a difference between being happy because you are doing something good, and being happy because you are doing things that make you happy for the moment, like movies and parties and such.

Anyway, Marcie asked over Joe (who I think might like me), Mollie, Ruthie and David. We spent all of Friday afternoon talking over what we could do.

David, the brains of the class — my old class, that is — says that we need to look at what has happened in Germany. He said that Hitler started off by comparing Jews to rats and vermin. He made Jews less than human and played on the old idea that Jews were ruling the world with their money and power. He turned them out of jobs and made them even more outsiders by making them wear yellow stars. So David thinks we need to do something right here, in Winnipeg, to educate students about prejudice, and to help them see that all people are equal.

And Ruthie thinks we need to raise money for the Red Cross and for Palestine. We can do that by having fashion shows and teas.

And finally, I think we need to do something about getting Jews here and not pay attention to the adults when they tell us to be quiet and not to rock the boat. I'm in charge of the refugees, David the education, Marcie the fundraising.

We needed a name so we came up with the Tikkun Olams, or TO's, because that means "to heal the world" and that's what we are all supposed to do, according to Marcie's religious school teacher, and that seems to fit our goals.

Elizabeth is sure to be angry with me for ignoring her all weekend. I'm not looking forward to school tomorrow.

I might have gotten a little overtired over the weekend. I'm feeling a bit off.

April 6

Disaster! Just when I have so much to do, I get sick! Dr. Borditsky just left. I have the chicken pox! And he says there's a good chance everyone I was with over the weekend will get it too, if they haven't already had it. I'm already starting to break out and I'm itching like crazy and I have a fever. I was so upset I cried and of course that made me feel worse. And Mommy has so much to do with the Red Cross, she goes every afternoon, and with Hadassah, she goes to meetings there in the morning, and now she is stuck home with me. She chided me, naturally, as she always does when we get sick. If I'd slept more . . . if perhaps I wasn't wearing my hat — as if that would have made a difference! — and I probably didn't eat properly when I was away (only Mrs. Grosman stuffed us with food all weekend, matzah French toast for breakfast, matzah ball soup for lunch, brisket for supper, and apples and stewed fruit all day long). At any rate, Martha offered to stay with me today; she was going to be here to clean anyway today and she offered to come in Wednesday and Friday, so Mommy will only have to be here Tuesday and Thursday.

I told Daddy about all the work I needed to do and he said that was perfect and that I could use the time at home to write letters.

LATER

I spent most of the day listening to the radio. I felt pretty sick all day and couldn't eat. I drank Coke and ate a little matzah, that's about it. Mommy says I don't have to keep Passover now that I'm sick but I want to. Daddy came home early with a big surprise. He'd stopped at the library and managed to get hold of four more Agatha Christie books. He also brought me the newspaper and read me the important stories. The good news is that 159 Axis planes have been shot down over the weekend. That's very good news. 300 bombers hit Paris and Cologne with 1000 tons of explosives. I hope that Sarah is safe! It must be terrifying for her.

I asked him if he thought Adam was back up in the skies and he said he thought the chances were good, but he knows that Adam wasn't on these flights because the names of the pilots were in the paper. Then he read me the rest of the article and after that he read me all the gossip from Hedda Hopper.

April 7

Daddy came home for lunch to check on me and he read me from my Agatha Christie, *The Body in the Library*. I think you must have to be a particular kind of person to write mysteries. You have to be willing to kill off all these nice people, for instance. I don't think I'd be able to do it. I asked Daddy if he could.

"Have a Girl Scout murdered in cold blood?" he asked. "No, not even if it was fiction. But you like to read about it, don't you?"

"I do," I agreed. "I love to try to figure out who did it. I don't like the murder part so much but I like it when the murderer is caught."

Then Daddy said something that made me think. "There's a sense of justice that is satisfied when the bad guy is caught. That's the real appeal, I think." He looked right at me. "It's why you want to do something to help your cousin Sarah. You want justice. You want fairness. You want your country to act the way things happen in books — where it all gets solved in the end."

He's right. I do. "But why doesn't everyone feel the same way?" I asked.

"Maybe they have a different idea of what justice means."

"Like Jews are bad people so it's a good thing to

keep them out of the country?" I asked him.

He looked sad. "I'm afraid that's the case."

That made me wonder if our government will ever agree to let Jews into Canada, no matter what we do.

I must have looked sad too, because Daddy added, "But that doesn't mean we stop trying. We can keep trying and putting the pressure on and doing whatever we can — what choice do we have?"

"I'll write my letters tomorrow," I vowed, "as soon as I feel better."

"Never give up, Devvy," Daddy said.

"I won't," I promised.

Daddy showed me an article in the paper about the Jewish community raising $8000 for medical aid to Russia. "It was your mother's committee who did that," he said proudly. "And you know that the Canadian Jewish Congress executive is lobbying the officials in Ottawa all the time. We just have to keep trying," he said, almost to himself, as if he'd forgotten for a moment I was there.

Martha put me in an oatmeal bath twice today and that's helped the itching; it's hard not to scratch, but I won't because I'll get scars. Mommy bought calamine lotion and I put that on often but the itching is almost unbearable. I can't even think about my letters yet.

April 9

There were big demonstrations by the World Jewish Congress, Daddy told me, all over the U.S. and Canada and here in Winnipeg. Mommy and Daddy went to a meeting and there was a press release, but no one seems to pay attention. Why?

Later

There is going to be a limit put on lipstick colours! Elizabeth called me after seeing it in the paper today. She was very upset! I laughed. She didn't think it was funny. I asked her if there wasn't something more serious to get worried over and she, in all seriousness, said no! And she said it wasn't only lipstick! It's face powder, and fingernail polish and they are even cutting off production of some face creams. Five colours, she says. What if one of those colours doesn't fit your face? We're too young for lipstick anyway, I told her. But she's mad on principle!

Meanwhile, Daddy read me the other important story from the paper — 36,000 men on our side might have been captured by the Japanese. But compared to lipstick, what does that matter? Honestly, I'm not sure how much longer I can be friends with Elizabeth. She's just silly.

Allan has just come down with chicken pox and it

looks like Hester got it first, so she must have given it to the rest of us. Turns out she had a fever and sore throat when she was at Elizabeth's during the snowstorm, but she was so keen to play that she refused to stay home. Thanks, Hester! For nothing!

April 10

I'm feeling much better today. I had a letter from the prime minister's office saying "my concerns are being looked at." But what does *that* mean? Probably that the letter will be put in a pile with other mail they don't care about.

I finished *The Body in the Library* tonight. What a surprise ending! As usual I was completely fooled! It made me think, though. Miss Marple is always talking about the little village she lives in and how there is evil there and that's how she knows so much about evil. Where does evil come from, I wonder? And if it's everywhere, like a village, or even a school, it must just grow so big sometimes that it takes over, the way it has now. But in crime novels, evil is always stopped. And we're trying to stop it in the world, with Hitler. But what if we can't? What if we lose? What if Hitler takes over and comes here and kills me and my family and my friends and even Jews I don't like, like Hester? And how did it get to this point, how did he get so powerful? I asked Daddy this when he came up to tuck me in. "When people don't stand up to evil it grows," Daddy said.

"But couldn't the German people tell the difference between good and bad?" I asked him. "Why didn't they know Hitler was — well, is — bad? Why did they hate Jews so much?"

"Well, Devvy," Daddy answered, "that might be two different questions. Sometimes bad looks good to people, especially if it seems like they are being offered a simple answer to their problems. In Germany, Hitler promised to get the economy working, to get people jobs, to get the trains running on time. And the Jews weren't really hated. They were judges and doctors and went about in society — they'd been there for a thousand years, after all. But Hitler needed a scapegoat and he chose the Jews. He started a campaign — first they were depicted as troublemakers and the reason for all the financial troubles; then they were depicted as less than human. And then Hitler made them wear stars so they were looked at as different than everyone else. And then he started to round them up and no one cared by then — or if they cared, they were too scared to say — and if they spoke out they were rounded up. They waited too long, and even the Jews didn't take it seriously."

"It's like Miss Marple says," I told him. "People don't see evil clearly. They're fooled. Maybe they don't have good enough imaginations."

"It's sad, isn't it," he said, "that we need to be able to imagine such bad things? But you are quite right, Devvy. Because refusing to see things only gets us in more trouble."

"When Martin stole Richard's pens last year," I said, "no one believed it even though Sandy had seen it happen, because they didn't think anyone in class would do that. And it was only when Mrs. Karlinsky actually saw Martin steal Marsha's scarf that they realized Sandy was right. And Martin is rich, he didn't need the pens — he was just doing it to have fun and to cause trouble because he wanted Sandy to get in trouble, because he liked her and she hated him."

"People like that must live very sad lives," Daddy said. "Imagine how they must feel inside all the time."

"But they make other people even more miserable," I said, "so I don't care how they feel. They never care about how other people feel. Hitler doesn't care, does he?"

"No," Daddy said, "he doesn't. But aren't you glad you aren't him?"

"Yes."

"Maybe you should read something a little more cheerful," Daddy suggested.

But I still have more Agatha Christies to read and I can't stop.

April 12

Sandy dropped over today to see me. She's had chicken pox already. Anyway, my scabs are almost healed now and I may be able to go back to school by Tuesday. She talked all happily about the news at school but I thought she seemed worried about something. Finally she blurted out, "My brother got a white feather at university last week!"

I was shocked. It's such an ugly way to accuse someone of being a coward — afraid to enlist.

"He really *wants* to sign up," she rushed on, "but the government won't let him leave medical school because they need more doctors overseas."

"People can be awful," I said, thinking of the talk Daddy and I had.

"He's so upset and ashamed," she whispered, and then she started to cry.

I gave her some tissues and then Mommy somehow popped up right at the perfect moment, and asked if we'd like to help her bake for the Hadassah tea. We jumped at the chance. We spent the whole afternoon with flour all over ourselves and we were able to lick the spoons after and Mommy told us stories about Palestine that she had heard from Auntie Adele who had been there before the war — she had actually snuck guns past the British. Mommy also told us funny stories about her Hadassah group, for instance how Mrs. Myers led the protest at City Hall when the men decided to blame the women of the city for clogging up the streetcars at rush hour with unimportant shopping, and how Mrs. Myers pointed out that the work at the Red Cross doesn't finish until 5 p.m. and would they rather the boys overseas didn't get their packages? And also that the women had to carry their own packages because deliveries are discouraged now, and how she got so mad that she had the women lay out their "unimportant packages" filled with food for their families' dinners and then she shamed the men at City Hall to carry them home.

It was a fun afternoon and I could tell Sandy felt better when she left. And it was fun to spend some time with Mommy.

April 13

Another letter from Sarah, again put into a letter Mommy got from Uncle Nathaniel.

Ma chère Devorah,
   I will try to write a more cheerful letter this time.

After all, what is the point of complaining? And what is there that either you or I can do? I wish I were Rachel's age.

What a wonderful time we had seeing our dear cousin a short time ago. He is so grown up, such a fine young man, and we were so proud to have him with us. That is, Rachel and I were. I'm afraid that my parents were a little worried. Silly. They worry about all the wrong things!

I hope you are well. I had a bad cough last week, but that is to be expected. We don't eat too well these days and we often feel weak. But I said I wouldn't complain! Please give my love to your dear parents,

Your loving cousin,
Sarah

I can see that she is trying to be more cheerful but has nothing to be cheerful about. We have so much space here in Canada. I simply can't understand why she can't come here. We would give them a home. We would take care of them. The government wouldn't be bothered by them at all! So why not? Only because they are Jewish? How are we any better than the Nazis who want to get rid of them? How? I just don't understand, dear diary, I just don't.

Daddy came home with a peach pie and two

lemon sponge rolls from the Grill Room for a dinner treat. I had a roll and a piece of pie. And Mommy made lamb chops for our dinner. Quite a feast!

Back to school tomorrow.

April 14

On my first day back I decided to try to do something useful for the war. So I marched into Mr. Joseph's office, and asked him if we couldn't copy what they are doing at Robert H. Smith, putting up flags from different countries in the morning instead of only the Union Jack. They've already put up the Czech flag and the Polish flag and next week they are going to raise Denmark's flag. He said he thought it was a good idea but that all the students should decide, and that if I wanted to change things there should be a referendum, which I should organize if I wanted the change. I said I would.

I told Mrs. Davis and she decided that the whole class should be involved. So I'm the chairman and I have to select a committee to oversee the referendum. Elizabeth wanted nothing to do with it and was really angry with me at recess. "What about our skipping competition?" she demanded. I assured her that it could wait. She sniffed and then said that she'd go ahead without me.

How mean! She could help me and then we could do the skipping. What's so important about skipping? She asked me what was so important about some stupid flags? Nothing, I guess, but it shows we care about the countries that are our allies. And we can educate students about our allies each week when we raise the flag and that might get them to help more in the war effort. They can raise money and collect things that are needed. So I told her that but she said I was becoming boring! And dull!

Sandy wanted to help and so did Hester. I'll have to get used to Hester talking non-stop, I guess. They will be my two deputies. And Paul also is on the committee as treasurer because we need to be aware of what the ballots will cost and we need to make sure everyone knows the issues. Marvin is going to be the secretary. The flags are expensive, but I checked already with the secretary at Robert H. and she says we can borrow one every week. And then we can make our own eventually, and that will also be a good project.

April 15

We spent the entire day organizing the referendum, which is to be held tomorrow. We went to each class, all four of us, and explained the question being asked. Then we left ballots, which say:

> YES, I want to add flags from other countries to the flag ceremony

> or

> NO, I only want the Union Jack.

Everyone has to circle one or the other.

APRIL 16

We won! By a landslide!

The four of us collected the ballots and counted them (missing boring geography), and every class voted in favour.

Tomorrow we'll hoist the first flag, the Czech flag. The school patrols will stand at attention. At Robert H. the cadets all line up but we don't have cadets here. And Peter will play the salute and the retreat at the end of the day on his trumpet.

Every day this week, practically, there've been pictures in the paper of Winnipeg airmen who have been killed in combat. Mommy wants me to stop reading the paper. She's threatening to stop getting it. She says I need to behave like a child and have fun. Have fun??

I remember it wasn't long ago when I worried that I had too much fun. How can she talk to me like I'm a child? I have two brothers in the war. Should I just pretend it isn't happening, like Elizabeth? (By the way, she stuck to me like glue all week, never letting me out of her sight and always making me play whatever the girls were up to. When I complained to Mommy, she said, "Why shouldn't you play? Will not playing make Hitler stop?" Well, I suppose it won't, but somehow it doesn't feel right. I did give in to Elizabeth in the end anyway, but I didn't have any fun! So there!)

Have I told you, dear diary, that the rivers are all swollen and there's been some flooding of basements already?

But something a little funny did happen at dinner. Daddy came home as usual about five and sat down to read the paper. Then his face got all red and he threw the paper down and swore! I've never heard him swear before! And Mommy looked at him with an amused sort of look and asked him what was the matter.

"It's madness! They're saying that they are going to let sheep graze on the golf courses! They want to increase wool production."

Mommy laughed out loud. Daddy is a championship golfer, but actually so is Mommy, and she has quite a few more trophies than he does. You'd never know it though, from the way he goes on and on about his golf.

"They'll keep the grass short and grow wool at the same time," Mommy said.

"And get in the way of my shots and make their messes everywhere!" Daddy objected.

He's funny. He's so calm about everything, but not about golf!

Actually it shows how busy he is — this is the first spring when golf isn't all we hear about. And Mommy seems to have forgotten about it altogether.

April 17

We came in third in the music festival today. Mrs. Foster was disappointed. I think she was hoping for first, but the other classes in our group were really good. It was fun and we got the whole day off school.

Tomorrow Marcie will meet me downtown. We're going to see *To Be or Not to Be* with Jack Benny and Carole Lombard. I wasn't sure I wanted to go. After all, it's a comedy and she's dead. It won't be funny to see her in all her beauty and to realize we'll never see her again after this movie. But Marcie just loves her and really wants to go. Typically morbid of her, but I said I'd go. We'll meet the rest of the TO's at The Chocolate Shop to plan our next projects and then Mommy wants me home — no sleepovers. She thinks I'm still weak or something. So far, none of the

TO's have caught chicken pox, thank goodness.

Other big news of the day — the boys in class are going mad with joy because the Toronto Maple Leafs have tied the series with the Red Wings, three all. Big game tomorrow and everyone will be glued to the radio.

Oh, and I forgot to report about the flag ceremony. It was so exciting and Mr. Joseph said he was very proud of the way the school voted. And he reminded us that in Nazi Germany they can't have any more elections, but that they did have one just before the war and that was when the Germans elected Hitler. He said that we need to always think carefully about what we vote for and never to take it for granted.

April 18

I'm glad Mommy didn't make me stop reading the newspapers. Today there was a full-page article all about Jews in Canada. And it didn't say one bad thing! I'm cutting it out and saving it.

The movie was swell, swell, swell. This group of actors has to outwit the Nazis. It's not exactly a comedy, more like a comedy and drama mixed together. I got so wrapped up I almost forgot the sadness of Carole Lombard's death. I ate too much popcorn and ended up in bed with the worst stomach ache.

I skipped ballet today because Mommy says I'm still too weak. I'm not weak at all. I'm all back to normal.

The stomach ache could also have been from the three cups of hot chocolate I had when the TO's met at The Chocolate Shop. David was mad at me when I told him what I'd done at my school. He said that education was his department. "But you aren't even at my school!" I objected. That didn't seem to make him feel better. But Marcie told him he was being silly and that what I had done was excellent and that they should do it at their school, so David said he would try to organize it.

I told them about the letter I'd written to the prime minister and the response which was probably nothing but some kind of form letter. Marcie reported that she was going to have a tea in two Saturdays and charge for drinks and baking and that we needed to get everyone to bake one thing and donate it. The synagogue will let us host it there. I told her she'd done a wonderful job! And as for David, he has written up an educational pamphlet describing what has happened to the Jews, and he wants to distribute it to all the schools in the city! That's a pretty high order but we all read it and it's excellent. I'm pasting it in here.

Judenrein

Judenrein means "Clean of Jews" and that is what Hitler and the Nazis are aiming for in Europe. It will happen here, too, should they win. But in the Aryan order it is not only Jews who are at risk. The Aryan model is based on pure blood and if your blood is not pure, for instance if you are Polish, or even black or any other race, you will be fit only to be a slave. But if you are a Jew you are fit for nothing.

We cannot let Hitler and his henchmen win! It is up to us to do whatever we can to help the war effort. We may be students but that does not mean we are unable to help. We can buy war stamps and war bonds. We can collect scrap. We can write letters to the troops. We can have fundraising events. We urge everyone to help!

In fact, Marcie told me that this week all the students from Aberdeen are collecting pots and pans and are going to a drop-off spot with them. She said it should be fun as long as it doesn't rain or hail or thunder. Trust Marcie to always think of the worst thing that could happen!

The Maple Leafs won the game tonight! There was lots of shouting from Daddy.

April 20

Horrible, horrible news from France. A thousand "Communists, Jews and sympathizers" were deported to Eastern Europe from Paris, and 30 hostages were executed because a troop train with Nazis on it was blown up by the Resistance. They are going to force French citizens to ride the trains with the troops so the Resistance will stop blowing the trains up, but I hope the Resistance will keep fighting no matter what. Mommy showed me a map and explained that France is now split into two parts, occupied France and unoccupied France. But the Vichy government in unoccupied France is collaborating with the Germans, so it is dangerous everywhere in the country. And the French are giving more Jews to the Nazis than the Nazis even want, according to Uncle Nathaniel in his last letter. He's become very discouraged. It's mostly non-French-born Jews being deported — so far the French-born Jews are not — but he doesn't know how long that will last.

Then Auntie Adele called, all upset. Cousin Jenny has signed up! She's joined the RCAF. Women won't fly, but will work on the ground as mechanics and such. She'll train at the university.

April 25

Back to ballet class today. Mrs. Roberts has announced our final presentation. It'll be short pieces she has choreographed, all based on spring. She began teaching us today. I'm in a group with Millie and Janice. Janice is better than me, Millie is worse. Then met Elizabeth for a matinee at the Uptown. We haven't been on very good terms, so when she asked if I felt like going I needed to say yes, or we'd be enemies instead of friends. I don't even know if I want to be her friend anymore, but I'm not sure I want an all-out war either. We went to the drugstore for soda afterwards and all she talked about was who likes who at school. Well, I didn't mind that. Naturally I'm interested — especially when one of the people she talked about was Paul! She's convinced he likes me. Well, I definitely like him.

Mommy cooked cabbage rolls for dinner tonight but I could hardly eat any because of all the popcorn and the sodas. All Mommy could talk about at dinner was the mosquito threat this summer. She's very worried and has told me I need to wear long sleeves and no shorts. I refused! She says 300 people had encephalitis last summer and that she doesn't want me to be one of them this year. Why does she have to worry about everything? The good news is there won't be a shortage of the oil that they use to kill the mosquito eggs. Because of the flood and all the water they're expecting a big "flight" by next week.

April 28

I forgot to write here about the conscription plebiscite that was held yesterday, but the results were announced today. A majority voted "yes," and by a margin of 3 to 1, though there were a lot more yes votes in English Canada than in Quebec. Mommy had done lots of work for it with her Jewish groups. It means that Mr. King can make conscription the law any time he wants to or needs to during the war. But at the bottom of the paper in a little box was an article saying that Canada was cutting all diplomatic ties with the Vichy government. That is good on the one hand because it tells them that what they are doing is bad, but on the other hand Daddy worries that they won't have any influence on the French now, and will that make it worse for Sarah's family.

May 1

Lots of big news today. First, Mommy got a list from the government about what kind of packages she can send to Morris. It must arrive in Ottawa before the 15th and she has dropped everything else for the next few days to get it organized. We are advised to send no food because Ottawa will be sending food and a new uniform for each soldier. But we can send a sleeveless wool sweater, toothbrush and tooth powder, safety razor and blades, strong soap (Mommy says it must be yellow soap), shaving soap and insect powder. Just being able to do something has cheered Mommy up and she spent the day shopping, but not all day because we have guests.

Mommy and Daddy's friends from Vancouver, the Mishimas, arrived today in Winnipeg. They are being sent out to a farm to live and work. It takes them away from the coast and at least they don't have to live in one of the camps for Japanese. So they are staying with us overnight. We listened to their story at dinner and I told them it sounded to me just like what was happening to Sarah's family. Why are they being punished just because they're Japanese? They are such nice people and they love Canada like mad. Mrs. Mishima cried a little and they were very tired and went to bed early. First thing in the morning they must be on a train that will take them out to a farm near Brandon.

May 2

It snowed today! Phooey!

That did not deter Mommy, though. She shopped all day for Morris. I shivered mightily waiting for the streetcar downtown and my ballet class. It feels colder when you have snow in May than when it snows in December — I wonder why. Oh well, at least we don't have to worry about mosquitoes yet!

The TO's got together today at the Met to see *Babes on Broadway*. The boys were very against it but Mollie and I insisted. I think the boys enjoyed it although they wouldn't really admit as much. It was wonderful — even though I've seen it once before. Judy Garland simply has the best voice in the entire world and Mickey is so cute! And it was labeled adult but we were still allowed in because my mother sent a note. I mean, how could they label a Judy and Mickey movie adult! Besides, from seeing it before, I knew there was nothing too daring in it. Though I think that's why the boys wanted to go — now they can boast they've been to an adult film.

Joe sat right beside me and bought my popcorn! He is pretty cute, I guess. Black hair, blue eyes. And he told some funny jokes. I didn't know he was funny.

We went to the The Chocolate Shop after for hot

chocolate and talked over our progress. We have received a good response to David's handout. Two schools are allowing us to give it out in the north end and this week I need to take it to the schools around my house. I'll do that this week after school. Or I'll try. I have extra rehearsals for the ballet show, my homework and now this! Of course I ate too much popcorn and drank too much chocolate and had a miserable stomach ache tonight. I know I shouldn't eat so much but I can never resist!

Next week *Fantasia* is opening. We've decided to meet again and see the movie first.

Daddy has joined a committee that deals with refugees and big Jewish problems in the world and now he's out almost every night at meetings. Twice last week I was home on my own. Daddy has told me that Mr. Blair is the government person in charge of refugees. He says that Mr. Blair hates Jews and everyone knows it. Why do Canadians stand for it? Why does this man, Blair, hate us?

May 9

It's been almost a week since I wrote here. I'll try to get all caught up. The ballet rehearsals are going well. The schools agreed to let us give out our handouts, but it takes us forever to copy them out and so far we've just made enough for four schools in all. As well as each of us copying, I still need to do my other war work like my knitting. Then there was school-work, and a game of Nazis versus us after school with all the kids on the block, when I wasn't at rehearsals. At recess we have a skipping marathon going as well. So you see, dear diary, I have been too tired at night to write. Today we saw *Fantasia*. What a show! I loved it. Joe sat beside me again and bought my popcorn again (yes, stomach ache) and told more funny jokes. He's talking more and becoming more interesting.

May 11

Mommy sent off the package for Morris today. She waited so long now she's worried it will be late arriving in Ottawa, so she sent it by special post. She kept collecting and knitting and adding until it was just perfect. We all added letters, of course, and finally Daddy forced her to send it!

I finished *One, Two, Buckle My Shoe*. It's the first Agatha Christie book I really didn't like. It was all about politics and I never got to care much about the characters, because we never really got to know them. I've started the last one Daddy brought me, *Hercule Poirot's Christmas*, and it's already very thrilling. The English people in the book don't take to foreigners. It's dangerous perhaps to look at people that way as a group — the way some people look at Jews differently.

May 14

A flyer who went to Kelvin High is missing. Big story in the paper today. Little time to write. Rehearsals for ballet every night this week. Show on Sat. afternoon.

May 16

I tripped and fell on stage!!

What a disaster! I was in the middle of this very serious part where the small birds are trying to survive an attack by a big bird, and we are whirling around and around and suddenly my foot just flew out and I was sitting there on the floor on my *tuchus* and just looking around without an idea of what to do. Millie reached down and pulled me to my feet and then whirled me around a few times while Janice danced alone, taking the attention away from me. Daddy told me that no one even noticed, but Mommy wasn't quite so kind. She laughed a little and said that failure is as good a teacher as success. Honestly! That may be true but it certainly didn't make me feel any less a fool!

We went to The White House for ribs afterwards though, and that took my mind off it for a while. But then I missed my brothers! It was their favourite place to eat. I'm going to sleep and hope that tomorrow will be a better day!

May 18

Letters today from Paris. Here's Sarah's.

Chère Devorah,

They have started to send people away in transports quite regularly now. Jews, of course. It is mostly the foreign Jews. People who came here to escape the Nazis in their home countries, or even people who came here twenty, thirty years ago. They are still considered foreign. Rachel and Papa argue almost every day now. She insists we must go into hiding. Papa thinks we are safer here because at least we have the proper papers and, not being foreign, we might be able to survive. I am torn, not knowing what is for the best.

I'm not sure that I have told you the circumstances we Jews live in these days. We were ordered to hand in our radios, then they disconnected our telephones, and then it became illegal for us to leave home between 8 p.m. and 6 a.m. And all the lawyers were arrested — all Jewish lawyers, that is. Papa was spared, but we aren't sure why. So you see, chère Devorah, why my mind wanders back to happy times.

Maman has confined me to the house when I'm not at school. We eat only the scraps that are left over in the few shops we are allowed to buy from, and with Papa unable to earn, we live on savings. I must admit I've turned into quite an accomplished piano player! With nothing else to do I practise all the time and am ready for my concert tour. I could never imagine such hardship happening here in my dear Paris, but it has. The packages your dear mother sends, even though infrequent, are such a help. Not only do they give us something to barter with, but just knowing that someone cares for us enough to go to all that trouble lifts our spirits so much.

Remember me with kindness, dear one, and try not to blame me for my miserable writings.

Love,
Your Sarah

I cried after I read that letter. I feel so frustrated and helpless. There seems to be nothing I can do to help her. I know I'm only eleven, but the adults don't seem to be able to do anything either. And I can't even write to her regularly because it is so hard to get mail smuggled to them.

Makes my little tumble in the concert seem silly now. I see why Mommy didn't take it seriously. With Morris and Adam and all of her family in France in real danger, a daughter tripping couldn't seem that important.

May 21

The British want to send up to 1000 planes at a time to bomb Mannheim, Germany. Did I write here that Adam is now a Flying Officer? Oh I wish I could be up there flying beside him! If we could only defeat Hitler right now, he and Morris would be safe and so would Sarah!

May 24

I've had to buckle down and study this past week. No movies this weekend, Mommy says. Exams next week and I'm a bit behind. Elizabeth has offered to help me study, which is very nice of her considering I've been spending much more time with the TO's than with her.

May 26

This in the paper today! Hong Kong Living Conditions Improve.

The paper said that reassuring news had been received concerning living conditions for military and civilian prisoners of the Japanese in Hong Kong. It said that conditions had been very bad — I dread to think! — but rations have improved and even some medicines have been provided. And mosquito nets have been supplied.

I can't stand the thought of Morris and Isaac suffering like that with no medicine or anything to protect them from the mosquitoes. If only we could hear if they are all right. I never want to say this out loud, but we don't even know if they are alive. There, I said it. I've been thinking that for so long now. Morris could be dead and we wouldn't even know it. There have been some families informed of deaths there, but we all know that with so little information . . . He could have died from starvation or disease or been murdered by a Japanese soldier!

If only we could have all been born at a different time, a time when there was no war and the only thing to worry about was getting good marks at school and things like that. Speaking of which, Elizabeth has been coming over to study every night after dinner. Mommy gives us a treat just before she goes home, hot chocolate and cake or cookies.

May 27

Forgot to mention that yesterday cuts in tea, coffee and sugar were announced. I'm not too bothered. It doesn't seem very important compared to everything else.

June 1

The entire city of Cologne in Germany was bombed, almost totally destroying everything and everyone there. All those people killed. But I can't feel sorry for them even though I suppose I should. Because if they hadn't blindly supported Hitler, well, he wouldn't have made this war, right? When I grow up I'm going to be very careful who I vote for and I'm never, never, going to just believe any old thing from my leaders. It's up to us to make sure these things don't happen, isn't it? Maybe I'll become a politician. I could. Girls can do anything now; the war has proven that.

I do feel badly about all those people. I do. And yet I'm so mad at them all. But the children aren't at fault, are they? I wonder how our boys feel? Do they feel sad about having to kill people, even children? They must. But they know that if they don't do it, it'll be their families who will be killed next.

June 4

Anna Neagle is coming to Winnipeg! It's hard to believe such a famous movie star is coming here in person, and guess where? The Uptown, right around the corner! AND, Daddy says that if I buckle down and study, he'll take me. There are going to be two plays and in between an air cadet tableau — it's to support the cadets. And there's going to be the RCAF band and an orchestra!

I'm going back to study now. Don't expect to hear much from me for the next few weeks. The TO's also have to finish up the work we are doing in schools so it's going to get pretty busy!

Mommy and Daddy are going to hear Louis Armstrong next week. Elizabeth is going to sleep over to keep me company, and we'll study.

June 6

A thousand planes attacked the Ruhr factories — the largest attack in history, the paper says!! And more good news — the Americans *crushed* the Japanese fleet when they tried to take Midway Island in the Pacific. Swell, swell, swell. We're beating them, that's what I think!

June 11

Britain and Russia have signed a pact. That has to be a very good thing.

June 12

Exams are over and I did really well! I got mostly As and two Bs. Today were our closing exercises and I got a special award for good citizenship because of my work on flags from the U.N. and the work we did on the flyers for the TO's. Mommy and Daddy were very proud of me. And I get to go to the Anna Neagle show!

Mr. Joseph gave an inspiring speech about the war and how we have a duty to the whole world to fight for freedom. He talked about the sacrifices that so many families in the school had made, losing sons in the fighting, or having them captured and having to live with the uncertainty, but said that we were all part of the war and we all had to sacrifice and suffer together. I could hear Mommy sniffling beside me, and most of the women had their hankies out by the time he was finished. I felt like crying but I didn't. Elizabeth was sitting beside me and I never would have heard the end of it.

June 15

ADAM IS COMING HOME ON LEAVE!!!!

In fact, by the time we got his letter he was already on his way!

June 23

Tonight we went to the concert. I know I haven't written but the house has been in chaos since we heard about Adam. Every single person we know has been calling and Mommy has been shopping and I've been helping her with the baking and the cleaning. As if Adam will care if there's a speck of dust in his room. I doubt his living quarters are that nice!

The concert was so wonderful. Miss Neagle was an inspiration. It was magical and even took my mind off Adam's arrival.

I don't think I'll sleep a wink tonight. Adam is coming in by train and gets here at 1 p.m. Daddy has cancelled all patients and Auntie Adele and family are meeting us at the train station. So is Baba Tema.

June 24

Woke up this morning to the horrible smell of oil! They have poured it all over the fields, which are just down the street from us, of course, and I know they need to do it for the mosquitoes, but did they have to do it the same day Adam's coming home?

LATER

Adam is here! I was the first one to spot him at the station and I ran like crazy and jumped up on him and hugged him so hard he even screamed! And then Mommy and Daddy and everyone else hugged him and everyone cried and it was such a wonderful moment I'll never forget it! Never, never!

And now that he's home I keep looking at him and staring as if I can't believe my own eyes. He looks so different. All grown up and older and very handsome! He's only going to be here for seven precious days though! Then he's going to speak at air force bases in Ontario and then back to England.

JUNE 25

Adam was on the front page of the paper today. A big article on all his exploits and a picture and everything! I tried to get it to paste here but Mommy put her foot down. She's getting it framed!

We're having a big party for him tomorrow with the entire family coming and then the day after another big party for all his friends who aren't overseas. Mommy made a brisket for dinner and a huge

chocolate cake for dessert and she used real sugar —
she didn't even care about rationing.

After dinner we asked him about what happened
when his plane went down and he told us how brave
Rachel is and how she's in the Resistance and how
bad it is in France right now. Germans everywhere
and people getting picked up off the streets and how
many Jews are being sent off.

Mommy made him go to bed early and get some
sleep, but before he did he came into my room and
tucked me in. I hugged him so hard it made him
squeak!

"If your other flyers could hear you now," I teased,
"they wouldn't think you are so brave." Then my eyes
filled up with tears and I begged him, "Don't go
back! Stay home with us!" and I threw my arms
around him again. He kissed me on the forehead and
then he said, "You know I can't do that, Devvy. Can
we let Hitler get over here? I know I might die. But if
we don't beat him we'll all die."

"You mean all Jews?"

"You bet I do."

"I know you're right," I said. "I want to do something too."

"But you are. The TO's are wonderful! You've
written to the prime minister. You're just a kid. You
don't need to do any more than that, Devvy." He

paused. "Well, maybe one more thing."

"What?"

"You need to be brave. Something could happen to me or to Morris."

"Don't say that!"

"But it's true. I face it every time I go up there."

"Aren't you afraid?"

"Terrified."

"How do you do it?" I asked.

"I don't know. The rituals, I suppose. Go through the same thing before the mission, and I remind myself why. And I'll tell you, Devvy, after being in France and seeing those Jerries first hand, well, they're a nasty bunch, that's all I can say and I think about that and that gives me the courage."

"Do you think Morris is all right?"

"He may not be the toughest guy in the world but he's smart. He'll figure out a way to stay alive if it's up to him. But Devvy, sometimes it isn't. It's in God's hands."

"God? God wouldn't let any of this happen," I said indignantly. "Maybe He doesn't even exist."

"I think He does, Devvy. Sometimes I'm up there in the clouds and flying high, looking at a sunset or at the sea beneath me and I swear I can see God all around. And when your mates put their life on the line for you and you see that kind of goodness you know He's there."

"But what about all the badness? What about Sarah? She might get killed because our country won't let her come here — for no good reason. Where's God then?"

"He's still here. But not everyone remembers He is."

"You've changed," I said.

"You too," he grinned. "You're a little lady."

I blushed and he kissed me goodnight.

June 26

YOU WON'T BELIEVE WHAT HAPPENED TODAY!!!!!
I FLEW!!!!!!!!!!!!!!!!

I'll try to start at the beginning although I'm still so excited I can barely calm down enough to write. Mommy had a big Hadassah meeting she couldn't miss and Daddy had his patients he had to see, because he's still catching up from taking the whole day off when Adam arrived, so Adam and I were left on our own. Mommy called school and told them that I wouldn't be in because I'd be spending the day with Adam. Daddy gave Adam the car and suggested we take a drive out into the country, maybe to the beach. So we decided to go to Winnipeg Beach for the day. But after Mommy and Daddy left, Adam got a call from a pal who is training airmen at Gimli, asking if he could come up for the day and show the young men a few tricks. Adam agreed and told me we could still go to the beach after. Honestly, I really didn't care about the beach, I just wanted to be with Adam and I told him so. Anyway, we drove up there in about an hour and a half. Mommy would have had a heart attack seeing how fast Adam drives! Haha. I loved it!

When we got there we met his friend John Peters. And that's when it happened. Adam looked at me and suddenly said, "Well, Dev, want to go up with me?"

He pointed to the plane standing on the runway. All the trainees were gathering round. John took off his jacket and gave it to Adam.

My heart was in my throat and at first I couldn't get any words out. "What say you, Devvy?" he asked.

I nodded, still unable to speak, not sure if it was pure fear or pure excitement or what I felt.

John grabbed one of the smaller fellows and commandeered his jacket for me. It came all the way down to my knees. I was also given a hat that covered my whole face just about and I must have looked pretty silly when I followed Adam to the plane. He hoisted me into the seat behind the pilot's, strapped me in, then scrambled up, and called over his shoulder telling me to sit tight. My heart was pounding so hard I thought it might explode right out of my chest and make a horrible mess and embarrass Adam.

I can hardly describe what happened next. The noise was so loud and we started to move and then we were up in the air. We flew up high and then came buzzing in right over the men waiting and then Adam started to weave and swoop. I think I was screaming most of the time but he just ignored me and I didn't mean it. I didn't want him to stop. Never, never have I experienced anything like it.

The main thing I noticed was just what he had said to me. Maybe that's why he took me. It was so beautiful. The sky was blue and there were little clouds and the ground below was green and I suddenly realized what Adam had been talking about when he talked about God. You just don't think or understand how much of a miracle this world is. How did it get made? How does it grow? How does life exist? Why? Why are we here? We're so busy living and taking for granted that we're living, but we never stop and think about how strange, how odd, how truly amazing it is that we live and we talk and we think, that we exist! And how truly wonderful it is.

I don't understand it at all but after being up there with Adam I have to think he's right. Maybe the bad people are like, well, like a good piece of cheese that's gone mouldy. There's nothing wrong with the cheese, but something goes wrong and it turns bad. There's nothing wrong with people, but something goes wrong, and people do very bad things.

When we landed Adam had to carry me off the field and sit me down in the grass for about a half hour while he talked to the troops and I recovered! By the time he was done I'd stopped shaking. On the drive home we agreed it would be our little secret. Mommy is never to know!

JUNE 30

Adam left today. I haven't written since our day out because it's been so busy. Every night a party. Mommy and me cooking like crazy. And then Friday was the last day of school. And Adam came to the flag ceremony and everyone cheered and cheered him. I was so proud!

When we saw him off I could hardly bear it. I didn't cry though. No one did. We knew it would be too hard for him if we did. Mommy warned me yesterday and we all managed to wave cheerfully as he left. But in the car on the way home I cried my eyes out. Mommy looked like she'd like to kill someone but I'm not sure who.

While he was here there was an article in the paper about three missing airmen from Manitoba and he knew all three. He feels bad being away from the fighting. He's going to Ontario to talk to the troops and then back overseas. Mommy packed a huge box of chocolate for him and his friends, and cookies and some new decks of playing cards.

July 2

Rationing is really and truly here now. Sugar ration cards were handed out today. And people have been hoarding for the last ten days knowing the cards were coming — including Elizabeth's mom, although I'd never tell on them. If I did they could be fined $5000!

Elizabeth and I are going to see *The Gold Rush* tomorrow. Can't wait.

July 3

It was so funny!! So funny!! Ate too much popcorn. Stomach hurts!!

July 5

Tomorrow I leave for camp. After Adam left it was a mad rush to get ready. I needed to buy all the supplies myself because Mommy was so behind in her Red Cross and Hadassah work that she had no time. Marcie and I did it together. Almost the entire TO's group will be at camp, everyone except Mollie. Elizabeth is jealous and can't believe that I'll be doing something fun while she's stuck in the city. Daddy had to put his foot down about my going. Part of me wanted to stay home in case I could do something for Sarah, but Daddy says I've done what I can and I need to get away and that not having me here will help Mommy get more of her work done so I have to go, and so I am!

More from Winnipeg Beach tomorrow!

JULY 20

I don't know where to start. I'm so sorry, dear diary, for forgetting you at home. I'm going to write down as much as I can about the last two weeks so I'll be caught up. It's mid afternoon and I'm sitting in the backyard. Elizabeth is coming over in an hour or so. Daddy picked me up at the train station because Mommy has a tea today. He's gone back to work.

Camp was wonderful, swell, sensational and altogether the best thing in forever.

I had my first kiss!

Joe kissed me on the last day. He kissed me right on the cheek. Don't know what I ever saw in Paul. Joe is so much cuter! If only he didn't live in the north end. But we are going to the movies together

— well, us and all the TO's. Marcie thinks I'm acting like a fast girl, letting Joe kiss me, but I think it was nice and I'll ask Mommy what she thinks tonight.

Anyway, it was so interesting. Young Judea Camp Kvutza. Naturally since it's a Zionist camp there was much discussion about Palestine. Maybe I'll go there when I'm grown up and work for the Jewish people.

I'll describe a typical day.

7:00 a.m. woken by the sound of a very loud whistle.

7:15 everyone is fighting at the washstands for a place.

7:30 mattresses aired out.

7:45 exercises. Mostly jumping jacks and touching toes.

8:00 breakfast! No, services first, then breakfast. Porridge, milk, bread, butter, jam, fruit juice. Always a fight for who gets the butter first, and then how much bread we can stuff into ourselves. Singing.

8:30 cleanup. I did the clearing away, Marcie washed dishes. Clean our tents.

9:00 morning *Sechot*. All of the TO's were in the same group, the juniors. Such interesting discussions. The Future of Jewish Youth. Arab-Jewish problem. Great Jewish Thinkers, etc. And all discussions came back to the purpose of the camp, Zionism. We even had Hannah Grossman, who has lived there, talk to us. Inspiring!

10:30 swimming!

12:00 lunch. Singing.

1:00 rest and mail. Elizabeth was very good about writing me and I'm very sorry for being so mean about her here in these pages. It's true, she isn't concerned about the same things that I am, but she's been a good friend. Daddy wrote me a couple times, Mommy once. I wrote them 4 letters. And Elizabeth daily.

2:00 *Sechot.*

3:00 swimming.

4:00 games.

5:00 rest.

6:00 dinner, wiener roasts, marshmallows, popcorn, (yes, many stomach aches) and then dancing the hora and singing until bedtime.

I'm so glad I went. It was so much fun and we talked about important things and yet somehow I didn't worry all the time. I could have stayed another two weeks.

LATER

So much has happened since I've been gone and now all the worry has returned. Mommy told me all of it at dinner. There has been an official report from Hong Kong about the prisoners. They say that conditions have improved and that the number of wounded has dropped from 1150 to 391 by the middle of March. They also say that the prisoners are satisfied with their food. But March is so long ago — what about now? I guess we'll have to wait another four months to hear about that! The chances that Morris or Isaac were wounded have to be pretty high.

There was some terrible trouble in Paris. Over 12,000 Jews rounded up on the 16th. I wish Sarah would write. Adam is back in England.

Oh how I hate this war!

Mommy says that there are 5000 Jewish children in France that the Jewish organizations are trying to rescue. They are lobbying the governments in Canada and the U.S. to get them out and are trying to arrange visas for them. But so far, nothing. Daddy is working very hard on it too. I said I wanted to help but they say there is nothing I can do, except not to mind if they are out most nights at meetings. Well, I can certainly take care of myself.

July 22

At dinner Mommy explained that they have been told that the French children they are trying to get visas for have been left in camps, their parents deported east. Both the American groups and Canadian groups are pressuring their governments. She is organizing a letter-writing campaign. Daddy's group is raising funds so they can show the government that they can care for the refugees.

Mommy read to me from an American Yiddish paper and I'm copying parts of it here.

Is it too much to hope and expect that these countries will open their door just long enough to admit the Jewish exiles at France . . . it's now or never. Either these Jewish victims hounded and persecuted beyond belief and imagination are now given a home in the countries beyond the seas . . . or the free world, when it rises on the ruins of war, will see only graves where living Jews with ability to create and desire to contribute to human happiness had roamed . . . Is it too much to ask that these children be given a new lease on life?

Surely the government will listen now. They have to!

July 24

Mommy came home in tears of happiness today. All the work she's done with her Hong Kong committee has paid off. We will soon be allowed to write the prisoners at Hong Kong and receive letters from them. Until we do I don't think any of us are really sure they are alive!

Went to see *Cowboy Serenade* today starring Gene Autry. Met all the TO's there and sat beside Joe. He bought my popcorn! Tomorrow we're meeting at the pool for a swim.

JULY 25

Bad news in the paper today about Hong Kong prisoners. Headline: POOR FOOD CAUSING WIDE-SPREAD DISEASE. It says that beriberi, pellagra, boils and dysentery are widespread and that some men have lost as much as 60 pounds. Mommy was pacing up and down the living room and *cursing*!

JULY 30

Elizabeth's basement flooded last night because of the horrible storm. We got some water as well and Mommy has been down there with Martha all morning, washing everything down with chloride of lime. She's had to throw out all her pickles, but fortunately the sauerkraut and jams were on a shelf in the garage and didn't get ruined.

What a storm! Lightning every few seconds and torrents of rain. I loved it. It was exciting.

There's a new Anna Neagle movie opening in a

few days. Of course we're all going. And the TO's have said that Elizabeth can come along.

July 31

A letter from Sarah. It's all too horrible.

Ma chère Devorah,
We are living in misery now after the horror that occurred in Paris. Let me tell you what preceded it, though. May 29 the Germans declared that all Jews here must wear a Star of David sewn to the outside of our outer garments — just like the Jews in Germany and other countries were forced to do. We had to pick them up at the police station and pay for it ourselves through our clothing coupons. It was yellow, outlined in black, the size of a man's fist, and the word Juif *or* Juive *written in black letters in the centre. I cried. But I had to wear it to school in June. I cannot tell you, my dear, the feelings I had when I walked into class that first day. Fear, humiliation. But Maman and Rachel told me to hold my head high, so I tried. And once at school, the principal made an announcement to the entire school that no one was to be treated any differently because of it and there was to be no teasing. But the looks of pity were so dreadful I almost might have welcomed a fight. Well, perhaps not. My friend Marie was not so lucky and*

at her school she was teased mercilessly and no one stopped it — the teachers seemed to enjoy it!

I cannot tell you how it made me feel after a while. I've never thought of myself as anything but French, just as I'm sure you think of yourself as Canadian. A Canadian who happens to be Jewish, yes? But when you need to wear something like that and it shows everyone that you are different, I just can't explain how you feel. Some in the city are supporting us by wearing yellow handkerchiefs and I saw a dog wearing a star on his lead! And when I travelled with Papa on the streetcar then people would get up and offer him a seat, just to show respect. But when the Germans noticed that was happening all over the city, they declared that Jews could only ride on the last car so then we couldn't even ride like everyone else. Less than six weeks after that, on July 8, we were banned from all public places, such as theatres and parks, libraries, museums, cafés, restaurants, swimming pools, even campgrounds. We can only shop between 11 and noon for food, between 3 and 4 for anything else, and by then the stores are picked clean. So no matter how difficult it was when school was in session, when it ended there was nothing to do and nowhere to go. I spend the afternoons in our courtyard with my friends, playing and trying not to think about the hunger *pangs. Rachel is always away.*

*And then it happened. On the 16th of July the
French police — not the Germans, the French —
rounded up thousands, thousands of Jews, most of
them foreign born. I must tell you that my friends
Martha and her baby sister Arlette are dead. When
the police came for them their maman pushed them
out the window and threw them to their deaths, and
then she followed. Maman didn't tell me — I found
out from my friend Alex. Martha was a year younger
than me and lived in a different area than us, but we
became friends through our piano lessons. She was a
true talent and made my playing seem babyish by
comparison. Her little sister was the sweetest child
you could hope to meet. It's true her maman was
high strung, but she used to say that she didn't want
her children to suffer and she would make sure they
didn't. We didn't dream that she would mean that. I
have not been able to shed a tear, I am so shocked. I
feel numb inside, dead.*

*The Jews they rounded up were taken to Drancy or
to the Vélodrome d'Hiver, a big sports stadium. We
heard the most dreadful stories from there. No facilities
for the bathroom, people trapped there for days with
no food or water and having to relieve themselves out
in the open and the stench and sickness. This in our
France! Again imagine it happening in Winnipeg and*

135

*you might have a small idea of the shock we felt. How
could our city have sunk so low? Papa seems to be in
some sort of trance, and barely speaks. Maman fusses
over him but to no avail.*

*We still hope to hear news of a visa or a way out of
here but hope is hard to hold onto these days.*

Pray for us.

Sarah

I showed the letter to Mommy and Daddy. Neither
spoke after they read it. Finally Daddy said, "It's as if
the darkest part of the human soul has taken over and
crushed anything good."

"Not crushed," Mommy said. "This is what happens when the worst in human nature is encouraged
instead of the best. But our side is encouraging the
best. We need to remember that, Devorah. Just remember that many people are fighting this evil."

Mommy had also had a letter from Uncle Nathaniel, of course, but she didn't tell me what was in it.
Something similar, I wonder, or just another fruitless
plea for help? I'm sitting here feeling so rotten I can
hardly describe it. I can't even think of anything to
write.

I just don't understand. I just don't.

August 1

The Anna Neagle movie, *They Flew Alone*, was inspiring. After the movie we went for ice cream sodas. I told the TO's about Sarah's letter. It upset them all and no one really knew what we could do about it.

Finally Joe said, "The best thing for us kids is to do what we can. We can't fight. We can't really make the grown-ups listen to us. But we can help in the war and that's what we should do, because the sooner Hitler is dead and defeated, the sooner Sarah will be free. So next year we should have as many fund-raisers as we can and do whatever else we can to help."

"I have an idea," Mollie said. "We could baby-sit for free after school so moms can go to meetings or if they need to do factory work." We all thought that was a grand idea and agreed to do it. We'll put notices up at the synagogue. And we'll continue David's education idea and we'll still do our own fundraising with teas and sales and we'll do our knitting.

I think we all felt better after. There's nothing worse than feeling helpless.

August 3

Daddy is on vacation this week and we're going up to Clear Lake until Sunday.

Later

We had a good drive. When we arrived we went straight to the lake and it was swarming with airmen who are here on leave. Auntie Adele and family are here too, including Jenny (allowed a week leave from training), and she's being mobbed by the flyers. No wonder — she's so pretty! There's a dance tonight and she says I can come with her.

August 4

I was too tired to write after the dance. I mostly just watched of course but occasionally a young fellow would let me dance with him just to impress Jenny. Mommy and Daddy came too and Daddy danced with me on his shoes. It was wonderful!

August 6

We spend all day at the lake swimming, or barbe-cuing at night, and we have to go back to the city too soon. There are lots of kids my age and we play all day together — made a new friend, Rosie. She's a year older than me and will be at Robert H. Smith next year in grade eight. She also has two brothers away and so she understands me and we can talk about our worries and it feels good.

August 9

We're back home. Busy every night playing a very long game of ring-a-levio and some of us are Jerries and some are Allies and it's been going on all week until all our parents call us to come in and then I'm too tired to write.

August 12

Saw *Mrs. Miniver* with Elizabeth. I cried my eyes out and to my surprise so did Elizabeth. All the way through you are sure that their brave son will die in the war, flying, and then a random bombing and his wife dies! Just like that. It was such a shock and I guess pretty true to life. The things you think will happen often don't, do they, and you worry and maybe you are worrying about the wrong things. Although in the case of Adam and Morris I think it's hardly worrying for no reason — or Sarah for that matter.

AUGUST 13

You won't believe this, dear diary, but I am writing from the train to Ottawa! I am so excited I can hardly hold my pen! Mommy just woke me up this morning and said, "I'm going to Ottawa to see what I can do about Nathaniel. Do you want to come with me?"

"Do I?" I exclaimed. "I'll say!"

"Well, you'd best get packing, the train leaves at noon."

And here we are. I'm sitting in the viewing car writing, as Mommy writes letters to Mr. Blair and his boss Mr. Crerar asking for interviews. She's also writing to the leaders of the Jewish Congress in Montreal to inform them about what she is doing.

At 4 o'clock we had tea in the dining car. It was so glamorous. White china and real tea, and little cakes. We sat with a young nurse returning to Toronto from leave in Winnipeg who will soon be going overseas again, and a young officer also returning from leave. He was stationed in England. He's in the navy, not a flyer, though, so he didn't know Adam. He too has decorations for bravery and I think he and the nurse hit it off!

Dinner was even more glamorous than tea. I dressed in my white dress with pink trim and Mommy put on her navy suit with the cream blouse, and we were seated with an elderly couple going to see their new grandchild in Ottawa, their son being away at the Eastern Front. Mommy did not tell them why we were travelling, she just said we had some business in Ottawa. I suppose she doesn't know who will look on our mission with sympathy and who won't.

We have a darling little room with bunk beds. I will sleep on the top. It's like some fabulous dream and part of me has to remind the other part that the reason for the trip is so serious because the other part is having so much fun!

August 14

We are staying in Toronto over the weekend spending time with people from the Canadian Jewish Congress — they have a regional office here, Mommy says. We're staying at the home of friends Mommy made doing her Hong Kong work. Their names are the Hamiltons and they live in Rosedale and it's the biggest, fanciest house I've ever seen. They aren't Jewish. Red brick, two stories, six bedrooms and we have our own bathroom attached to our guest bedroom! They have a son in Hong Kong and a daughter two years older than me, who has not been very friendly since I've arrived. Her name is

Corrine. She's a real snob. We had a very fancy dinner and there were so many knives and forks, I had no idea which one to use, so I watched Mommy; she seemed to know what to do. We ate four courses and they had servants serving us. First there was clear soup, which I hated but forced myself to eat. Then there was fish — also disgusting so I mashed it around my plate and made it look like I'd eaten it, and then these little birds called Cornish hens that are impossible to cut up and a wing went flying up and hit me in the nose, but everyone pretended it hadn't happened. If it had been at my house I would have been teased for weeks!

AUGUST 15

We went to Spadina and College and met a bunch of Mommy's friends for deli. Now that's a meal! Oh boy, the food was delicious. I had a huge pastrami sandwich and a huge pickle and a huge piece of apple pie for dessert.

The adults talked for hours and it got pretty heated. After about an hour they all just kept repeating the same things. Some thought Mommy shouldn't be doing what she was doing and that she should be leaving it to official channels, and some thought that it couldn't hurt because both Crerar and Blair were refusing to meet with the officials from the Congress.

I got very bored with all the details and asked permission to walk outside. Mommy said I could so I walked down Spadina and looked in the stores and bought little presents for my friends. I bought two scarves, one for Elizabeth and one for Marcie, and they were only 25¢ each! The street was packed with people, as were the shops. It was very exciting.

AUGUST 16

We've arrived in Ottawa and have checked into a hotel downtown. We ate at the hotel dining room and it was very elegant. The train ride here was crowded, full of people who had been visiting Toronto for the weekend and now have to return to work in Ottawa — as well as troops, of course. I stood for much of the trip, as there was always an older person who needed my seat. Of course I offered before I was asked.

AUGUST 17

What a horrible day. Mommy had word from the secretaries of both men and they have both said they will not see her. She decided to go their offices, but that was fruitless. We sat in the waiting room of first one, Crerar, for three hours and then the other, Blair, for four hours! I thought I would die of boredom and at one point almost broke into Blair's office by force, but the secretary was a man who looked strong and ready to lift me and throw me out if he had to.

Mommy wrote letters, again, to them both as we sat there and asked the secretaries to show them the letters. They agreed and then the same thing happened in both offices. They came out, said the letters had been read, there was no point in waiting, that they would write her if there was any change in policy, otherwise there was nothing that could be done. Mommy actually then tried to get into Mr. Blair's office but she was barred by the secretary standing in front of the door. So Mommy said to him, "I hope, sir, that when the war is over we will all be able to say that we were proud of our actions during such a trying time." He went pale and said, "I hope so, too." But wouldn't budge.

Finally we came back to the hotel, tired and discouraged.

August 18

We are back on the train to Winnipeg. We left Ottawa early this morning and connected to the Winnipeg train after lunch. Mommy told me that we mustn't be too disappointed because we tried our best and that's all we can do. But I am! And I'm mad! Why couldn't they have at least seen us? It would have been only a few minutes of their time.

August 19

Daddy is very happy to have us both home. And I'm glad to be back! It was a real adventure, but somehow it seems all spoiled now because we didn't accomplish anything. Daddy says we tried, and that's the important thing. But Sarah couldn't see it that way, could she?

There is a big battle going on in France at Dieppe. Dieppe is on the French coast and there are many Canadians on the ground. One thousand planes are trying to shield them and I'll bet Adam is up there, maybe even now. The papers say that the Germans have lost over a million troops in Russia. I'm glad they are on our side now — the Russians, that is.

August 20

I went to see *Mrs. Miniver* again today with Marcie. She loved the scarf. She says I should be happy I got to do something and that it was nice that Mommy asked me along, and that it probably helped Mommy to have some company and that I shouldn't expect anyone to change. But I do! Why can't they change?

What is the matter with grown-ups? I hope when I'm older I'll always keep an open mind.

But I am proud of Mommy for trying. She's a grown-up who tries her best, that's for certain. And Daddy too, of course!

AUGUST 21

A wire from Adam saying he is safe. Lots in the papers about how brave the Canadians were at Dieppe. The Brits are saying it was Canada's greatest day of the war, the greatest air scrap since the Battle of France, and the U.S. is saying the same thing — and as usual that means Adam!!! The pilots in the paper say it was a tremendous dogfight and a flyer is quoted as saying that they really gave it to Jerry. But Daddy says there have been many lost.

LATER

Lists of dead from Dieppe and pictures in the paper's front page of Manitobans who died. Marcie's cousin is one of the dead. She's been crying all day. So many died! And so many others wounded. If that was a success, I'd hate to see a failure — that's what Mommy said at dinner tonight.

August 26

I know I'm not writing very much, but this week we played until very late every night — and then I'm too tired to write. Tonight there was an eclipse of the moon and the whole gang from the street watched together. Have I said who's been playing? Sandy, Mary, Elizabeth, Paul, John, Hester.

The Duke of Kent, the king's younger brother, died in a plane crash. Even being royalty won't save you.

We're starting junior high soon. I'm a little nervous.

August 29

MORRIS IS ALIVE and has sent us a letter! A LETTER! The most amazing, fantastic, wonderful, spectacular, stupendous news!

One beautiful page.

Mommy won't let me put it in here so I'll have to summarize. He says he is fine and that he is tanned! And that Isaac is fine too and that they received tooth powder and other things and that we shouldn't worry about him, but to take care of ourselves and that he hoped to write once a month. And that he is being treated well and that they play volleyball and basketball and bridge!

This is the best day ever — except for the day Adam came home!

AUGUST 31

Most horrible letter imaginable from Sarah.

Ma chère Devorah,

I wonder whether it is worth going on. Everything seems so black. Our neighbour, Mme Bresson, volunteers at the Drancy prison trying to help the poor unfortunates held there. She came to have tea with Maman the other day and I overheard their conversation. I wasn't meant to, but with nothing to do anyway, I just sat on the floor outside the parlour and listened out of sheer boredom. What I heard!

Remember I told you of all the Jewish families that were rounded up in July? Well, after being held in the sports arena and various places they were sent off to camps. The authorities did not yet have permission to deport the children to the east, but they did not want to delay the trains so they sent the adults. Parents were separated from the children with no mercy — apparently it was heartrending. The adults were sent to Germany, she thinks. Children from two to sixteen were left behind with no one to care for them. Finally the children were packed onto trains and sent to Drancy where she encountered them. Oh,

Devorah, how can people be so cruel? And French people? These were not Nazis, these were French organizing these transports.

The children had travelled for days and nights all alone without parents, one or two adults to each cattle car. The older children helped the younger ones when they got off the trains, some carrying the babies in their arms. When they arrived at Drancy they were covered in insects and their clothes were soiled, and smelled. They were covered in bruises and impetigo. Mme Bresson had to tell them they would be reunited with their parents. They showed her pictures of their parents if they were old enough. Most of the children had diarrhea and dysentery and for a bathroom only a rusty can. They slept on straw on the floor. She and her fellow volunteers tried to get them food but there was so little to go around. Two days later, the gendarmes began to ready them for the trip east. The French guards ripped any bracelets or jewellery off them, even earrings, tearing them out of their ears. Some child called the place they were going "Pitchipoi" and for some reason, soon they all began to call it that. They would say, "We'll see our parents soon, in Pitchipoi."

At 5 in the morning they were awakened and somehow they knew and did not want to go to the courtyard and they started to cry. So the gendarmes carried them down as they screamed in terror. And then they were taken away. Mme Bresson went in the buses with them and saw them packed into sealed cattle cars.

I never let on that I heard because Maman said, "We must not let the children hear about this. They will be too frightened."

Now I see why Martha's maman threw her out the window. How she knew what was in store I cannot guess. Perhaps she only guessed or had heard from others, but I am glad Martha died quickly with her family. But to be glad of such a thing, you can see how far we have sunk. So I ask again, why go on? I've been feeling rather unwell, but it is probably the result of the lack of food. Your packages are all that keep us going, I think.

Your dear cousin,
Sarah

I showed the letter to Daddy. He looked very sad after he read it. "These must be some of the children we wanted visas for so we could get them over here," he said. "That they should have met such a fate!"

"Why are people so cruel?" I asked him.

"Another big question," he replied. "Maybe they each have a different reason. One person does it because he enjoys it, one because he's afraid to say no, one for power, one because he actually believes he is doing the right thing."

"How could anyone believe that kind of cruelty is *right?*" I asked, and he said, "You can convince yourself of anything. But if people followed Hillel's advice, they would be far better off: Treat others as you would wish to be treated. That's basically what Hillel said. And when you think about it, Devvy, if we all did that, the world would be a much better place."

I'm very worried about Sarah. She sounds like she's given up hope.

LATER

One hundred and twenty-two families received letters from Hong Kong. Today pictures were in the paper and the names of those whose families received letters, including Morris.

There were more casualty lists from Dieppe. The number of dead, wounded and missing is so high and I feel so badly for those families getting bad news. I've looked through and see that many of them live around here, so when school starts tomorrow there are bound to be lots of very sad students.

I'm a little nervous about starting a new school and wonder who will be in my class.

September 1

First day was pretty good. There was a very emotional assembly where Mr. Bruce talked about those sacrificing so much, so that we could be free. There was a moment of silence and we all said The Lord's Prayer and sang "God Save the King" and marched outside to raise the flag.

Then we were sent to our new rooms. Elizabeth is in my room and so are Paul and Hester, Sandy, Mary — too bad — and actually I won't write them all down here, but it seems like a good class. Our homeroom teacher is Mrs. Clark. We go from class to class now and that will seem strange. The school is very busy with war work, much more so than Grosvenor was. The boys can join the cadets and the girls can help with projects, like knitting, collections and such. I feel better about that. It means I won't have to separate all the war work from school as much as I did last year. But they expect more from us now we are in junior high.

I write Sarah once a week and Mommy collects the letters and then sends them whenever she mails her parcels, but today I wrote an extra letter. I urged her to keep hope alive. The war can't last forever and we are making headway against Hitler. She just needs to remain strong. I worry though, because she is so sensitive and has such a kind heart. She must find this kind of inhumanity more than she can stand.

September 3

A letter today from Uncle Nathaniel. Sarah is very ill with pneumonia. He asked if anything was being done about the visas. Mommy has written him back.

She told him about our Ottawa trip and how she's tried everything and just doesn't know what else she can do. She told him that he has to consider what to do without thinking about a visa because she truly doesn't think that he will get one. She had to tell him the truth.

September 4

More numbers of wounded and missing are coming in from Dieppe and it looks as if Mommy might be right — how could it be called a success if so many men died or were wounded or taken prisoner?

There's a beef shortage developing but Mommy says that we can't spend time worrying about that when there are really important things to worry over — and at least that means fewer cabbage rolls!

September 11

A twister came to ground outside the city today near Boissevain. In the city we had a pretty scary hailstorm and lightning crashing all around. I love storms. I turn out all the lights and watch the lightning from the living room window. After it was over I felt as if I'd forgotten something but I couldn't think what, and then I realized that it was strange to not be worrying about the war and Morris and Adam and Sarah even for a few minutes. I'd forgotten to worry!

September 12

The whole family got together tonight at Auntie Adele's for New Year's. It's 5703 in the Jewish calendar. The adults talked non-stop about the refugees and what the Congress was doing and what they were doing. Cousin Jenny let me walk around in her high heels and try on her lipstick and powder. Mommy will have everyone over for Yom Kippur.

September 15

Dieppe casualties, 3350. That includes missing and wounded. Hester has a brother missing. Marvin has a brother who's been wounded, and there are at least three people from other classes who have lost family — two were brothers and one was a father.

September 21

Yom Kippur. We went to services today and last night. We don't often go, but Daddy suddenly wanted to so we went to the Shaary Zedek in the north end. I wore a little grey skirt and white blouse and black patent shoes and Mommy wore a new hat and a brown suit. Most of the TO's were there and we went out during the sermon and hung around outside talking. It was a nice day and the leaves are turning. Joe seemed very surprised to see me and quite pleased. I actually enjoyed the service. I read along in English and found it interesting. I don't have to fast until I'm 12, but Joe was fasting and so was Marcie. They didn't look like they were having too much fun. Mommy never fasts, Daddy always does. Mommy says she doesn't feel she needs to fast to be a good Jew and it makes her feel sick, and why would it make her a better Jew to feel sick?

September 29

Sarah is dead.

September 30

Sarah died of pneumonia.

I think she died of a broken heart.

Hitler killed her. He might as well have shot her in the head.

Uncle Nathaniel wrote on the twelfth with the news. But we just got it. All that time when I was happy and celebrating the New Year and going to synagogue and thinking about silly things — all that time she was gone. Gone.

Dear diary, you know I tell you everything, but how can I tell you something I don't know? And I can't describe to you how I feel. No one close to me has ever died before. Shouldn't I be crying and wailing and screaming? I haven't even cried or anything. It doesn't even feel real to me. It's like a bad dream and I'm sure I'll wake up and everything will be all right. And since I haven't seen Sarah in so long, I can't grasp that this isn't just the same — I can't see her now, but soon I will. Maybe my heart is made of ice.

October 1

I am still numb from the news about Sarah. Mommy has suggested I have a memorial service for her on the weekend. I don't want to do anything. So

Mommy came into my room tonight and gave me quite a talking to.

"Do you want Hitler to win?" she asked me.

"Of course not," I said.

"Then don't let him. He's killed your cousin. He might yet kill your brothers. And you've let him kill your spirit."

"Gloria," Daddy said, "Don't be so hard on her. She needs to grieve for her cousin."

"She needs to fight!" Mommy said. And she stalked out of the room.

Oh yes. The parcels for the Grenadiers have arrived at Hong Kong along with medicines, cigarettes, dehydrated vegetables and fruit juice. I'm relieved to think of Morris getting some of the things they need so badly.

OCTOBER 3

Today was the memorial service for Sarah. All the TO's came and so did Elizabeth and Sandy and Paul. I gave a speech. This is more or less what I said:

"My cousin Sarah was a very special person. She played piano so well and was so talented that one day she probably would have played in a symphony and become famous. She was kind and she was sweet. She loved to eat — especially big thick sandwiches and

French fries from Kelekis. But even if she had been a bad person with no talents, she didn't deserve to die just because she was Jewish. No one deserves that. I don't know why people love Hitler and follow him. I don't know why people hate Jews. It makes no sense to me and I don't understand it. I just wish that this wasn't happening because I'll miss her so much." And then there was more I wanted to say but suddenly my throat felt like it had closed up and I couldn't speak.

Joe came over to me and took my hand and looked in my eyes and said that he was very sorry she had to die and suddenly it hit me, really hit me, that I would never see Sarah again or even get a letter, no matter how miserable she sounded, and that she would never return in any way. How can death be so final? And so quick? I started to cry and couldn't stop. I ran into my room and flung myself onto the bed and I cried and cried and cried. Mommy came up and hugged me and I wept in her arms until she wiped my face with her handkerchief and sent me back out to my guests. Then she brought out cookies she had made and also her special chocolate cake using all our sugar rations and I think chocolate must be like medicine because I actually felt a little better after I ate.

Elizabeth thinks everything is good and happy, Marcie the opposite. Since this has happened I've been thinking a lot about it. Is the world a good place, I mean basically good? Or is it a bad place? I mean really bad? I need to ask Daddy. And I need to ask Adam. Will write him tonight.

October 5

I've gone from not being able to cry to crying all the time. If I hear something sappy on the radio or am reading a book, or anything, I'll burst into tears. It's happened twice at school. Elizabeth, thankfully, isn't telling me to buck up all the time. I feel better when I'm doing the war work at school. But not much better.

St. Louis Cardinals won the World Series today. It's all the boys could talk about at school, who would win. And I think a few skipped school to listen to the game because attendance was down. I know Joe told me he was going to be "sick" today.

October 17

Today was my birthday, as you well know, dear diary. I didn't want to do anything for it, but Mommy arranged a party for me. She invited all the TO's and Elizabeth and Sandy. She took us to see *Footlight Serenade*, with Betty Grable, at the Capitol. Then everyone crammed into the car and came back home for a dinner of hot dogs and fries and ice cream and cake. I tried to have a good time because I didn't want to disappoint anyone, especially Mommy, who had gone to all that trouble. Sometimes I found myself crying because Sarah will never have another birthday. Sometimes I had fun and then I felt guilty.

I asked Daddy whether the world was a good place or a bad place. He says good will always triumph over evil. But why do so many have to die for that to happen? Why can't we have a world where good wins before millions of people have to die? How can I live in a country where so many are willing to sign up and fight and die and they are so good and noble, and yet our very own government won't let in a few Jews and so they die and no one cares about that. It doesn't make sense. We are fighting against Hitler and all his racial laws, but then we have all these hatreds right here in this country. I wish I understood. Maybe when I get older.

October 19

The official list of prisoners of war from Hong Kong was released from Ottawa today. And there was Morris's name in the paper, along with Issac's. Daddy suggested to me that I should be happy for such good news, but how can I be when any moment the news could be bad?

OCTOBER 21

During dinner Mommy and Daddy were unusually quiet. After we'd eaten Daddy asked me to sit with him in the living room. I started to get nervous. Daddy cleared his throat. "Devvy," he said, "Auntie Aimée finally had the courage to go through Sarah's things. When she did she discovered a letter Sarah had started writing to you right before she died." He picked up a piece of paper from the side table. "Auntie Aimée sent it to you." He passed it over to me without another word. I took it and went to my room to read it. Here it is.

Ma chère Devorah,

I know that I am very ill. Should something happen to me, I hope you will not despair, but that you will carry on working to help end this horror. I feel that I am enveloped in blackness and that if I die, or when I die, only then will I feel warmth, see light, and be happy. Perhaps then I will be able to play music and run freely and laugh out loud for no reason. Perhaps then I will be able to hug the friends I will never have and to kiss the children I will never have. Perhaps then . . .

October 22

I couldn't go to school today. I stayed in bed. I couldn't eat. I couldn't listen to the radio. I can't even write in these pages.

October 23

Daddy keeps wanting to talk to me but I just stick my nose in a book.

November 1

I know I haven't written, but I haven't been able to. I go to school and I come home, but I feel like nothing matters anymore. I don't care. The world is a bad place, a very bad place. Sometimes I wish I could die and be with Sarah. Yes, diary, I do!

November 2

A letter from Adam just for me. Remember I asked him about whether the world was good or bad?

Dearest Dev,

What hard questions you ask, little sister. I have thought quite a bit about life and death, though, so I do have some things to say to you. Every day I see men take off from these airfields and every day I see

some who return and others who don't. Do I think
God decides who should live and who should die?
Although many people believe that, and believe that
there is a reason for everything, I can't accept that. It
just seems to be luck, nothing more. After all, what is
the reason for an innocent child like Sarah dying?
Surely God isn't punishing her. And I don't believe
He is punishing the Jewish people for not following
His path. Such a God would be like a cruel and
demanding parent. I can see why people thousands
of years ago believed that, but in this modern age I
find it hard to swallow.

So if there isn't a reason for God to take these lives,
why do people die? Is it all for nothing? Is there no
rhyme or reason in this life?

I think, Dev, it's up to us to find a reason. Maybe
Sarah didn't die because God wanted her to. Maybe
she died because Hitler wanted her to. God has given
us free will and so many have made the wrong
choices over the last few years.

And now to your big question — is the world
friendly or is it unfriendly? Dev, I have my opinion,
but you'll have to decide that for yourself. Just think
about this question. How does everything grow?
Where does life come from? Here's a hint: love!

As you know, I saw Sarah in person not that
long ago. She was a lovely child. Very sensitive.

And she played piano like an angel.

She had a good friend in you and I know that meant a lot to her. And you had a good friend in her. So you were both lucky. Do you think Hitler has any really good friends?

Love,
Adam

NOVEMBER 5

I've spent the last few days thinking about Adam's letter and his question to me, *How do things grow?* I don't know! It's such a mystery, isn't it? I asked Daddy. He gave me a scientific explanation. I asked Mommy. She said she was too busy to think about such things. So I sat in the backyard after school, staring at the withered flowers and looking at the yellow leaves on the ground. Everything in the world grows. But Daddy's science only goes so far. What made the science? God? And is God everywhere? And is that what Adam meant by love? Does he mean that love makes everything grow?

That would mean that the world is a good and friendly place, not a mean and cruel place, even though mean and cruel things happen in it. I guess I'll never know for sure, but I can decide what I want to think about it. And it seems to me, diary, that life won't be so hard and miserable if I look at it from the good side instead of the bad side. Elizabeth does it naturally, but she tries to pretend the bad doesn't exist. That's a mistake, I think. And Marcie will occasionally be happy but mostly she won't be, will she? So maybe there is a middle way and maybe that'll be my way. There are people who act out of love and there are people who don't and I guess whatever happens, I'd rather be the kind that acts from love. I'm lucky. People who act from hate must be so miserable and they make others so miserable and thank goodness I can choose not to be like them.

I've filled up almost this whole diary and soon will have to start a new one.

I can't stop bad things from happening. But I'm named after a fighter, Devorah from the Bible, and I'm going to fight, just like her, and do everything I can to help win the war. If I don't then Hitler wins, doesn't he? I mean, if he can make me so sad and mad that I don't care enough to fight, he's won and I've lost and Sarah died and nothing matters and something has to matter. Something has to matter.

Maybe this will be the last war ever. When people see how bad it is, maybe . . . or maybe there will always be people who want wars and there will always be people who have to fight them. That would be sad, wouldn't it?

EPILOGUE

Devorah and her friends, the TO's, continued to work until the end of the war for the war effort. They were always at the forefront of school projects and also created their own projects, such as free baby-sitting and educational pamphlets. They stayed friends through high school and through college, and even after they were all married they would get together at least once a month for dinner. Often they would meet in the summers at Assiniboine Park for picnics with their children. They referred to each other as "the gang."

Devorah also remained friends with Elizabeth, who became a doctor — quite unusual for a woman at that time. She looked after Devorah's children, coming to the house any time there was a problem. Elizabeth had no children of her own but took care of many.

Adam was injured on D-Day, June 6, 1944, and sent home. He lost the use of his left arm. Because of his actions during the D-Day campaign he was awarded another bar for his Distinguished Flying Cross. He spent the rest of the war at bases in Manitoba, where he trained other airmen.

Morris returned home at the end of the war, but Isaac did not. He died of abuse at the hands of the Japanese. Auntie Adele never recovered from his death.

Jenny served in the Women's Division of the RCAF in England and married a man she met there, Frederick, who was a pilot like Adam. He turned out to be from the gentry and lived on a huge estate. Auntie Adele and Uncle Simon moved to England and lived on the estate so they could be close to their grandchildren, Jenny's twin boys.

Morris went back to school and became a psychiatrist. After the war ended, Adam also went back to school to study engineering; he became a professor at the University of Manitoba. They both married and each had three children. All the cousins would get together every Sunday, eat deli and sometimes talk about the war. But not often.

Devorah was always devoted to her brothers, never forgetting how lucky she was to have them both survive the war.

The Jewish refugee children in France were never given visas by the Canadian government. They were sent to Auschwitz, where they were gassed. Sarah's family did survive in Paris, because the French Jews were not specifically targeted the way foreign-born Jews were. Rachel was captured by the Gestapo, and tortured, but managed to escape. She later married and had six children. She said she had a few extra to make up for the ones Sarah would never have.

Devorah grew up to be a determined fighter for right. She went to college and graduated in political science. She married Joe, who became a lawyer; together they had three children. When the children were young she was a stay-at-home mom, but always busy with volunteer work. When they got older she ran first for school board and won, then for parliament and won. She went to Ottawa and worked hard on issues near and dear to her, especially human rights. And she made a difference.

Devorah named her first child, a daughter, Sarah.

HISTORICAL NOTE

The Second World War began in September of 1939 when the German leader, or Führer, Adolf Hitler, invaded Poland. But Hitler's war against the Jews started when he seized control of Germany in 1934. A series of discriminatory laws designed to isolate German Jews and portray them as undesirable were followed by direct attacks such as the November 1938 *Kristallnacht*, or night of broken glass. That night, Hitler's Nazi thugs burned synagogues and attacked Jewish-owned businesses throughout Germany. The following day 30,000 Jews were arrested and taken to a new concentration camp at Dachau, as well as to Buchenwald and Sachsenhausen.

Canadians were deeply moved by news of the *Kristallnacht*. Large rallies of concerned citizens gathered in Winnipeg, Toronto and other cities to express their outrage and to urge their government to change its immigration policies that denied Jewish refugees entry to Canada. Canadians had long practised or accepted their own forms of antisemitism, limiting the access of Jews to universities, some professions and many private clubs, but Hitler's violent racism shocked most Canadians. Unfortunately, Prime Minister Mackenzie King refused to order his officials to admit Jewish refugees, so nothing was done to alter Canada's record as the country in the Western world that admitted the fewest Jews fleeing Europe.

With the outbreak of war, Canadians enlisted in large numbers. By the spring of 1945 more than one million men and women, from a population of eleven million, had volunteered for service in the army, navy, air force or merchant marine. Under the British Commonwealth Air Training Plan, tens of thousands of Canadian and Allied airmen learned to fly at bases in Manitoba, such as the one at Gimli, not far from Winnipeg, and in other Canadian provinces.

After the defeat of France, Canada became Great Britain's most important ally in the war against Nazi Germany. Most of the Canadian army and air force was sent to Britain, while the navy and merchant marine concentrated on convoying goods to Britain across the North Atlantic.

In June of 1941 the war was transformed by Hitler's invasion of the Soviet Union. The early successes of the German army in Russia encouraged the Japanese Empire to make preparations to wage war in the Pacific. British, Dutch and French colonies were to be conquered and the threat of American intervention dealt with by a surprise attack on the main American naval base at Pearl Harbor in Hawaii.

The governments of Britain and the United States tried to persuade Japan to avoid war, both through diplomacy and also by making military preparations that they hoped would dissuade the Japanese from further action. American bases in the Philippines were reinforced, Australian troops were sent to defend Singapore, and Canada was asked to send a small contingent of several infantry battalions to reinforce the British and Indian troops at Hong Kong. The Canadian government agreed to send the Winnipeg Grenadiers and the Royal Rifles from eastern Quebec to join the Hong Kong garrison, in the hope that a show of strength and solidarity would help to avert war. This decision was a serious mistake, as Japan had long since decided on war. After a brief, valiant struggle, Hong Kong surrendered. Canadian casualties were 297 killed and 493 wounded. Another 264 Canadians died while prisoners of war. Of the 1975 Canadians who sailed from Vancouver in 1941, just over 1400 made the voyage home when the war ended in 1945.

During the winter of 1941–1942, Canadians were playing a very large role in the Battle of the Atlantic and the air war. After the German invasion of Russia began, Britain and Canada tried to send supplies by convoy to northern Russia, and also sought to draw the German air force away from Europe's Eastern Front by air attacks on Germany and German bases in France. Royal Canadian Air Force fighter pilots were active throughout 1942, serving in the British Royal Air Force, as well as RCAF squadrons such as No. 402 City of Winnipeg Squadron. This unit was converted from Hurricanes to the faster Spitfire fighter aircraft in March of 1942. Adopting the motto "We Stand on Guard" and a badge with a grizzly bear, the squadron was involved in the largest single air battle of the war, which took place during the tragic Dieppe Raid on August 19, 1942. On D-Day (June 6, 1944), No. 402, along with other RCAF and RAF fighter squadrons, played a major role in the successful invasion of Normandy and the liberation of Europe.

Canadians also contributed large numbers of men to RAF Bomber Command. More than twenty percent of all its aircrew were Canadian, and in 1943 most of the Canadians were concentrated in No. 6 Group RCAF, which flew four-engine Halifax and Lancaster Bombers in the strategic air offensive against Germany.

By the end of the war, sixty million people had died. Canada lost forty-five thousand in the struggle to destroy what Winston Churchill called "a monstrous tyranny, never surpassed in the dark, lamentable catalogue of human crime." But these numbers cannot begin to tell us the real stories behind every death, behind every act of courage, and about those who fought the war from their homes as best they could.

Canadians (and, at that time, Newfoundlanders, since Newfoundland did not join Confederation until 1949), have much to be proud of in the role they played in World War II. However, what Canadians might well wish we had done differently during those years, if we had the chance to go back and change our actions then, concerns a major chapter of World War II: Hitler's "final solution" to rid his country, and its "master race," of Jews.

On June 14, 1940, Paris, the capital of France, fell to the German army. On June 22, 1940, France signed an agreement with Germany stating that Germany would occupy the northern part of France while the southern part of France would remain unoccupied. In the unoccupied part of southern France the town of Vichy became the centre for a new French government. The Vichy government promised to cooperate with Germany. Marshal Henri Philippe Pétain became head of state of the new French government. Officially Vichy claimed to be neutral, but that was not what happened.

Almost immediately they began to pass antisemitic legislation. In October of 1940 they passed the first *statut des juifs*, Jewish law, and the second in June of 1941. These laws gave the government a legal foundation for their persecution, excluding Jews from the army, the professions, commerce and industry, the civil service, and from public life in general. Jewish-owned property was confiscated. Foreign Jews were rounded up and sent to internment camps. In the latter part of 1942, the French police, not the Germans, rounded up mostly foreign Jews in the occupied and unoccupied zones. By the end of 1942 over 40,000 Jews had been deported, most of them ending up at Auschwitz–Birkenau, where they were murdered. By 1944, 77,000 Jews, most of them foreign, had been deported from France and killed. In the meantime, thousands of French Jews went into hiding or tried to escape to Spain and Switzerland. Many joined the Resistance and fought the Germans until the end of the war.

This brings us to the Holocaust. Jews had lived in Europe for over two thousand years, and unfortunately they were often the victims of a hatred called anti-semitism. Raul Hilberg, in *The Destruction of the European Jews*, describes the six stages Hitler used to destroy the Jews: definition, expropriation, concentration, mobile killing units, deportation and finally, killing centres. The Jews were defined by the Nuremberg Laws passed in Germany in 1935 — if one of your grandparents was Jewish then you were Jewish. Then Jewish people were stripped of their property, businesses and homes. After that they were sent to live in ghettos, small areas (often in cities) where a few city blocks held thousands of people crowded together, starving and being forced into slave labour.

The mass killings began in 1941 after the invasion of the Soviet Union. Entire populations of towns and villages were rounded up and shot. However, for Hitler this method was too slow, and too hard on his troops. So in 1942, at a conference of Nazi leaders held in Wannsee, a suburb of Berlin, a new policy was put in place. Jews would be sent to centres where they would be killed in mass numbers and in a more impersonal way. The concentration camp, initially set up as a prison camp and a slave labour camp, ultimately included killing centres as well. Jews were not the only people sent to these camps — trade unionists, clergy, political enemies, male homosexuals, gypsies and mentally and physically challenged Germans were also killed.

What was Canada's reaction to the terrible things happening to the Jews in Europe? Politically — complete indifference. In fact, in their book *None Is Too Many* Irving Abella and Harold Troper argue that Canada actually had the worst record of allowing

Jews into their country of any nation that could have invited them in. Even Chile and Bolivia took in 14,000. Canada, from 1933 to 1945, allowed in only 5000! This record is truly shameful. The U.S., for example, let in 200,000 Jews — a stunning difference.

The Liberal Party, led by Mackenzie King, came to power in 1935. Head of the government's immigration branch was Frederick Blair. His section was placed in the Department of Mines and Resources headed by Thomas Crerar. But Crerar was not interested in the immigration issue at all, so Blair had total power over all decisions related to refugees. It was unfortunate, to say the least, that he didn't like Jews. He was an antisemite, and acted as if it was his personal task to keep Jews out of Canada.

Canada's Jewish community tried their hardest to change the government's policy and to convince political leaders that Jews were in mortal danger. But Mackenzie King's government, supported by Blair's tactics, made sure it never became an "issue" the government had to deal with. The Canadian population, particularly in Quebec, was not eager to see Jews come to Canada, and Mackenzie King's government did not have the political will to change or challenge public opinion, even if there were individual politicians who were more sympathetic to the plight of Europe's Jews. Unfortunately, the Jewish community was tiny — only around one percent of Canada's population — and they had little political clout. They tried hard to lobby and change minds, but in the end the prime minister's delaying tactics were too much for them, and they were able to accomplish very little.

One of the most tragic threads of Canada's record on allowing refugees to immigrate — and there are many — is that a number of Jewish children who were "cleared" to come out of Vichy France never made it safely here because of Canada's stalling. Most were sent east to concentration camps and died there. Only 2500 of the 77,000 Jews rounded up in France survived. A new Holocaust memorial, a "Wall of Names," was opened in Paris's Jewish quarter in January of 2005. It has taken over half a century for the French to fully own up to their role in sending so many Jews to their death.

Winnipeg Grenadiers march down Main Street, Winnipeg, in 1939.

Canadian airman at the Elementary Flight Training School at Portage La Prairie, Manitoba.

A *mother saying goodbye to her son on June 5, 1940,
as he and other Winnipeg Grenadiers head for the
West Indies. In the train doorway (right, upper) are
two brothers who survived internment in Hong Kong.*

If Day: February 19, 1942. Winnipeg stages a mock invasion by Nazi soldiers, to promote the sale of war bonds. Here, men acting as Nazi soldiers burn books outside the Carnegie Library.

Mock Nazi soldiers give their typical salute as they ride tanks down Portage Avenue in Winnipeg during the staged invasion.

Lieutenant-Governor R.F. McWilliams of Manitoba, and other dignitaries, are led past the buffalo monuments in the legislative building during the staged invasion of Winnipeg on If Day.

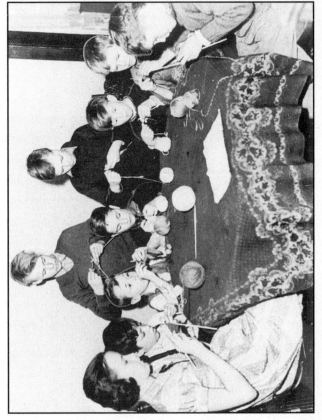

On the home front, children knitted squares to be sewn into blankets for the troops, as part of the war effort.

Children collected scrap metal, such as pots and pans, in aid of the war effort.

The six-pointed Star of David, which Jews in France were obliged to wear on their clothing, with the word Juif or Juive for "Jew" spelled out. French Jews over the age of six had to wear the Star of David.

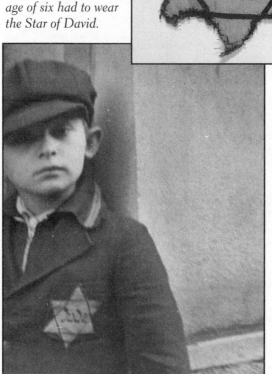

A young Jewish boy in Prague, Czechoslovakia, wearing the obligatory Star of David sewn onto his jacket.

ÉTAT FRANÇAIS

TRAVAIL — FAMILLE — PATRIE

PRÉFECTURE DE POLICE

DIRECTION DES AFFAIRES ADMINISTRATIVES DE POLICE GÉNÉRALE — SERVICE SPÉCIAL

ORDONNANCE

relative au

CONTROLE DES JUIFS

Paris, le 10 Décembre 1941.

NOUS, Préfet de Police,

Vu :

1° La Loi du 2 juin 1941 remplaçant la Loi du 3 octobre 1940 portant statut des juifs;

2° La Loi du 2 juin 1941 prescrivant le recensement des juifs;

3° La Loi du 22 juillet 1941, relative aux entreprises, biens et valeurs appartenant aux juifs;

4° L'Avis du Commissaire Général aux Questions Juives;

ORDONNONS :

ARTICLE PREMIER

Les juifs des deux sexes, Français ou Étrangers, seront soumis à un contrôle périodique.

Les modalités de ce contrôle, portées à la connaissance des intéressés par voie de presse, ou sous forme de convocations individuelles, devront être strictement observées.

ARTICLE 2

Les juifs domiciliés dans le département de la Seine devront, dans tous les cas où ils seront appelés à justifier de leur identité, présenter leur carte d'identité délivrée ou visée par la Préfecture de Police, postérieurement au 1er novembre 1940 et portant, de façon très apparente, le cachet « Juif » ou « Juive ».

ARTICLE 3

Les juifs venant de province devront, dans les vingt-quatre heures de leur arrivée dans le département de la Seine, se présenter en personne à la Préfecture de Police, munis de leurs pièces d'identité, livret de famille et pièces attestant leur situation militaire.

ARTICLE 4

Les juifs changeant de domicile, même à l'intérieur du département de la Seine, devront en faire la déclaration, dans les vingt-quatre heures, au Commissariat de Police du lieu de départ et à celui du lieu d'arrivée.

Des autorisations de déplacement hors du département de la Seine (à l'intérieur de la zone occupée), pourront être accordées par la Préfecture de Police, dans des cas graves ou exceptionnels.

ARTICLE 5

Les personnes juives ou non juives qui hébergeront des juifs, à quelque titre que ce soit, et même gracieusement, ou leur loueront des locaux garnis ou nus, devront faire au Commissariat de Police une déclaration spéciale, indiquant le nom, prénoms et état civil complet des intéressés, ainsi que le numéro, la date et le lieu de délivrance de la carte d'identité présentée. Cette déclaration devra être faite dans les vingt-quatre heures de l'arrivée du juif ou de la location.

ARTICLE 6

Les biens appartenant aux juifs ne pourront, en aucun cas, être transportés hors du département de la Seine.

ARTICLE 7

Les changements survenus dans la situation familiale (naissance, enfants atteignant l'âge de 15 ans, mariage, etc...) devront être signalés à la Préfecture de Police.

En cas de décès, la carte d'identité du défunt devra être remise au Commissariat de Police.

ARTICLE 8

Les personnes qui ne se conformeront pas aux prescriptions ci-dessus seront passibles des peines de droit sans préjudice des sanctions administratives.

Les juifs, notamment, pourront faire l'objet d'une mesure d'internement.

ARTICLE 9

Les Agents de la force publique sont chargés de l'exécution de la présente Ordonnance qui sera imprimée et affichée dans Paris et dans toutes les communes du département.

Par le Préfet de Police :

Le Secrétaire Général,   Le Préfet de Police,

DAUDONNET.   **BARD.**

Paris. — Imprimerie CHAIX (Succursale B), 11, boulevard Saint-Michel. — 2144-44.

La législation antijuive de Vichy est une création spontanée, hors de toute pression des autorités d'occupation. En 1942 et 1943 le recensement des juifs par les services de Darquier et Pellepoix sera utilisé par les Allemands pour « la solution finale ».

The announcement by the French government detailing antisemitic legislation, Paris, December 10, 1941.

Gendarmes in Paris round up French Jews for questioning, 1941.

Non-French-born Jews in the Austerlitz train station in Paris, with their few possessions, awaiting deportation to internment camps.

Mothers and children outside a building in an internment camp in France.

Canadian prisoners of war at Sham Shui Po Camp, thin and weakened, soon after being liberated following the fall of Japan. Some POWs were used as slave labour in Japanese shipyards.

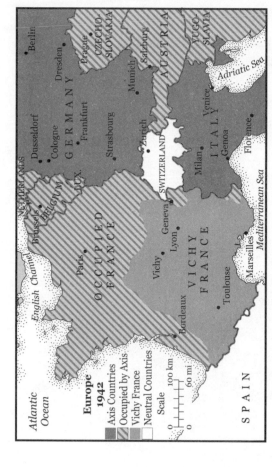

Map of Europe in 1942, showing the Axis countries, which were at war with the Allies. Northern France was totally occupied by the Germans; southern France was not. Jews in both regions of France were severely persecuted.

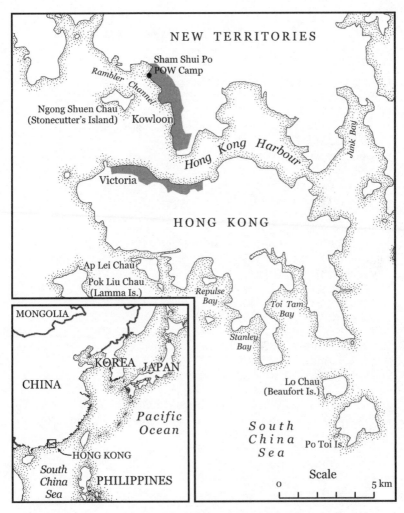

The region of Hong Kong included Hong Kong Island, as well as the New Territories north of the city of Kowloon. Many prisoners of war were held at the Sham Shui Po POW camp.

ACKNOWLEDGMENTS

Grateful acknowledgment is made for permission to reprint the following:

Cover Portrait: Detail, adapted, from the Canadian Jewish Congress Archives, Montreal.

Cover background: Detail, lightened, from photograph of a German SS soldier supervising the deportation of Jews in the Krakow ghetto, Poland; the United States Holocaust Memorial Museum, courtesy of Archiwum Documentacji Mechanicznej, 02159.

Page 178: Western Canadian Pictorial Index, A0594-18674.

Page 179: Western Canadian Pictorial Index, A1281-38353.

Page 180: Western Canadian Pictorial Index, A1279-38312.

Page 181: Western Canadian Pictorial Index, A1290-38618.

Page 182: Western Canadian Pictorial Index, A1290-38624.

Page 183: Western Canadian Pictorial Index, A1290-38627.

Page 184: Western Canadian Pictorial Index, A0025-00742.

Page 185: Western Canadian Pictorial Index, A1234-36952.

Page 186 (upper): United States Holocaust Memorial Museum, courtesy of Claudine Cerf, N09426.

Page 186 (lower): United States Holocaust Memorial Museum, courtesy of Czechoslovak News Agency, 77929.

Page 187: United States Holocaust Memorial Museum, 89793.

Page 188: United States Holocaust Memorial Museum, courtesy of the Bibliothèque Historique de la Ville de Paris, 81034.

Page 189: United States Holocaust Memorial Museum, courtesy of the Bibliothèque Historique de la Ville de Paris, 79929.

Page 190: United States Holocaust Memorial Museum, N02830.23.

Page 191: Library and Archives Canada, PA-151738.

Pages 192 and 193: Maps by Paul Heersink/Paperglyphs.

Dr. Irving Abella, co-author of *None Is Too Many*, shared his expertise on the Holocaust and the Jewish refugee situation during World War II. Terry Copp, author of *No Price Too High*, lent us his keen military eye and generously assisted with the Historical Note. Barbara Hehner carefully checked the manuscript and particularly assisted regarding World War II pilots. Michael Nathanson and Rebecca Brask not only produced the most beautiful grandchild in the world, but also spent hours in front of microfiches, copying a year's worth of *The Winnipeg Tribune*, and helping with the research. Per Brask listened to the manuscript and gave me invaluable encouragement. And finally I cannot even describe everything my editor Sandy Bogart Johnston accomplished — three weeks working with me to track down whether mail could go back and forth between Paris and Winnipeg, helping to choose and acquire pictures, and oh yes — editing the book. My heartfelt thanks to all of the above.

I would also like to thank the Canada Council for the Arts for the grant which allowed me to take the necessary time to fully research this book.

For my new grandson, Zevi Joseph Nathanson.
With love from your Safta.

ABOUT THE AUTHOR

Carol Matas's parents were born in Canada, but her grandparents and great-grandparents immigrated here from various eastern European countries. It was fortunate for her that they were not among the thousands of Russian and European Jews seeking to come to Canada during the horrifying events of World War II — they might very well not have been able to emigrate. Carol's father was unable to fight in the war because he had health problems, but one of her uncles fought in India. One of Carol's cousins was in the Winnipeg Grenadiers and — like Morris and Isaac in this story — was a prisoner in Hong Kong until the end of the war; another cousin, Sam Sheps, died fighting in Europe.

During the war, when Carol's mother was sixteen, she played piano for children at a child-minding centre, while their own mothers were at work. Carol says, "Many of the events in the book are taken from stories she told me, as well as stories my cousins Mark Bernstein and Babs Asper told me about their life at school during the war years in Winnipeg."

Carol's first Dear Canada book, *Footsteps in the Snow: The Red River Diary of Isobel Scott*, was nominated for the Silver Birch Award and the McNally Robinson Book of the Year for Young People Award. Carol is one of Canada's leading writers of historical fiction, and is best known for her books about the Holocaust, such as *Daniel's Story* (shortlisted for the Governor General's Award and winner of the Silver Birch Award), *After the War* and *The Garden* (both winners of the Toronto Jewish Book Award), *Lisa* (a Geoffrey Bilson Award winner), *Jesper*, *Greater Than Angels* and *In My Enemy's House.*

Carol has written books set in other historical periods too, such as *Rebecca* and *The War Within*, as well as contemporary stories like *The Lost Locket*, fantasy and science fiction, and thrillers such as *Cloning Miranda*, *The Second Clone* and *The Dark Clone.*

Carol lives with her family in Winnipeg, Manitoba. One of her resources for *Turned Away* — apart from regular research, personal interviews and the rereading of numerous Agatha Christie mysteries — was the old microfiche files of *The Winnipeg Tribune* from the war years. That made, she says, for some interesting decisions while she was writing the book, since headlines of the day might not always accurately reflect what we know today. During World War II, ordinary citizens had to rely on newspapers and radio for news of the progress of the war. Today, individuals can also gather additional information via the Internet, but even so, stories change as more information becomes available. Now, as during World War II, claims are sometimes made, even by major news sources, that later turn out not to match up with hard fact. But the headlines of the day are what people know on that day, and Carol wanted Devorah to be responding as a twelve-year-old Winnipeg girl in 1941–42 would have.

Carol says, "When I discovered If Day, I was amazed. Winnipeg became quite famous for its re-enactment of the Nazi invasion and was emulated by other cities all over North America. It was a chilling reminder — arrests, book burnings, the seizing of all media outlets to control the truth, and even control over everything that happened in the schools.

"We owe the deepest dept of gratitude to those who gave their lives in order to defeat the worst examples of humankind. And personally I can never forget that had I lived in Europe, my voice would have been silenced along with those of two million other Jewish children. That is one reason I feel the need to give a voice to those, like Sarah in my book, who were silenced forever."

Library and Archives Canada Cataloguing in Publication

Matas, Carol, 1949-
Turned away : the World War II diary of Devorah Bernstein /
Carol Matas.

(Dear Canada)
ISBN 0-439-96946-8

1. Jewish children–Europe–History–20th century–Juvenile fiction.

2. Canada–Emigration and immigration–History–20th century–Juvenile
fiction. 3. World War, 1939-1945–Juvenile fiction. 4. Jewish children in
the Holocaust–Juvenile fiction. I. Title. II. Series.

PS8576.A7994T87 2005   jC813'.54   C2005-901409-1

6 5 4 3 2 1   Printed in Canada   05 06 07 08 09

The display type was set in WurkerCondensed.
The text was set in ElectraLT Regular.

✻

Printed in Canada
First printing June 2005

✻

Dear Canada

Other books in the series:

A Prairie as Wide as the Sea
The Immigrant Diary of Ivy Weatherall
by Sarah Ellis

Orphan at My Door
The Home Child Diary of Victoria Cope
by Jean Little

With Nothing But Our Courage
The Loyalist Diary of Mary MacDonald
by Karleen Bradford

Footsteps in the Snow
The Red River Diary of Isobel Scott
by Carol Matas

A Ribbon of Shining Steel
The Railway Diary of Kate Cameron
by Julie Lawson

Whispers of War
The War of 1812 Diary of Susanna Merritt
by Kit Pearson